ANNO[...]G ORANGE™

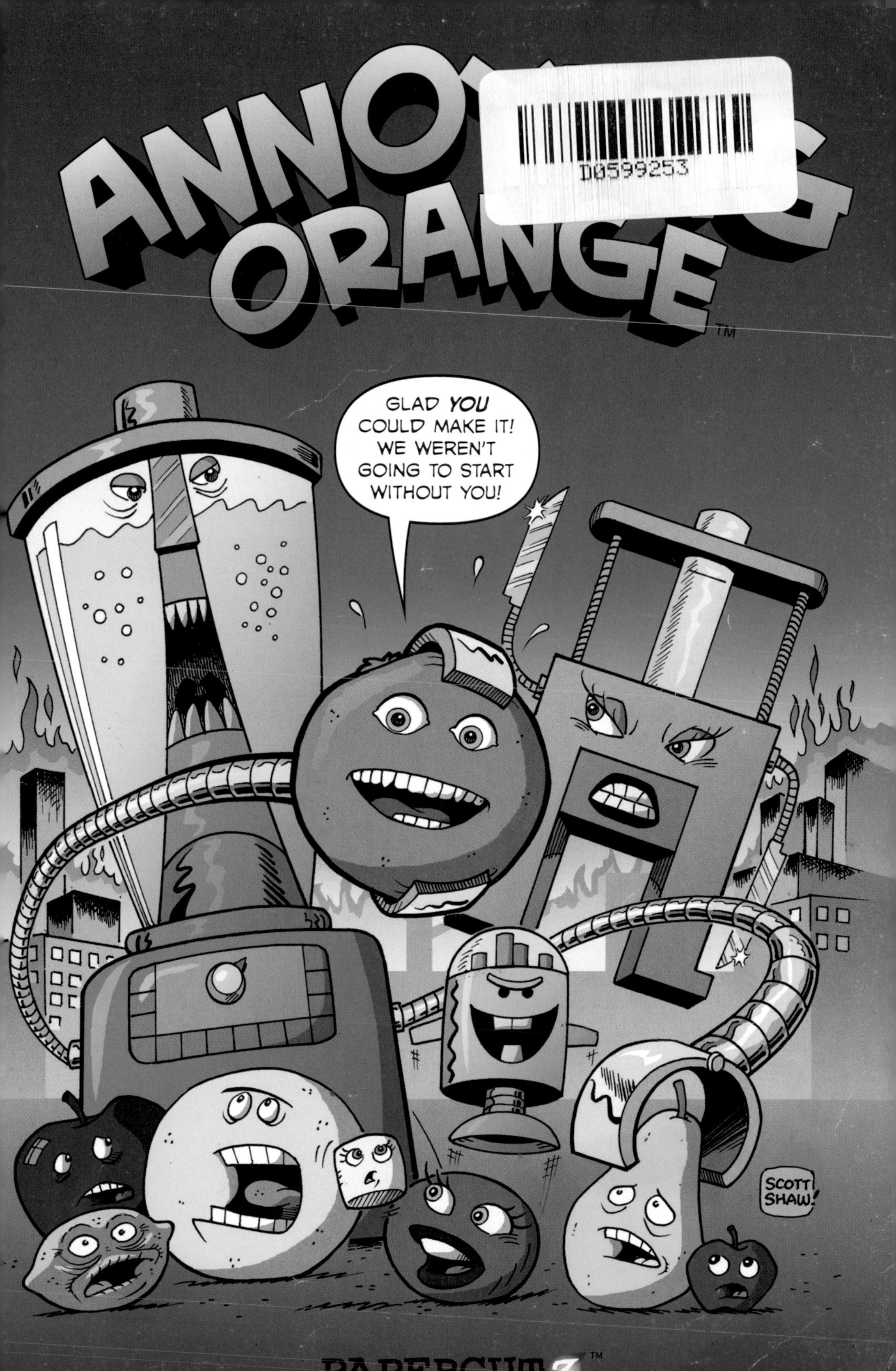
GLAD *YOU* COULD MAKE IT! WE WEREN'T GOING TO START WITHOUT YOU!
SCOTT SHAW!

PAPERCUTZ™

ANNOYING ORANGE™

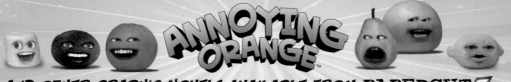

AND OTHER GRAPHIC NOVELS AVAILABLE FROM PAPERCUTZ

COMING SOON!

ANNOYING ORANGE
SECRET AGENT ORANGE!

ANNOYING ORANGE
Graphic Novel #1
"Secret Agent Orange"

ANNOYING ORANGE

ANNOYING ORANGE
Graphic Novel #2
"Orange You Glad You're Not Me?"

ANNOYING ORANGE
PULPED FICTION

ANNOYING ORANGE
Graphic Novel #3
"Pulped Fiction"

ANNOYING ORANGE
TALES
CRISPER

ANNOYING ORANGE
Graphic Novel #4
"Tales from the Crisper"

ANNOYING ORANGE
TRANSFARMERS

ANNOYING ORANGE
Graphic Novel #5
"Transfarmers: Food Processors in Disguise!"

ANNOYING ORANGE
Little Baloney

ANNOYING ORANGE
Graphic Novel #6
"My Little Baloney"

PAPERCUTZ SLICES
Harry Potty

PAPERCUTZ SLICES
Graphic Novel #1
"Harry Potty and the Deathly Boring"

PAPERCUTZ SLICES
breaking down

PAPERCUTZ SLICES
Graphic Novel #2
"Breaking Down"

PAPERCUTZ SLICES
PERCY JERKSON

PAPERCUTZ SLICES
Graphic Novel #3
"Percy Jerkson & The Ovolactovegetarians"

PAPERCUTZ SLICES
THE HUNGER PAINS
PETRUCHA
PARKER

PAPERCUTZ SLICES
Graphic Novel #4
"The Hunger Pains"

PAPERCUTZ SLICES
THE FARTING DEAD

PAPERCUTZ SLICES
Graphic Novel #5
"The Farting Dead"

The Three Stooges
BED-BUGGED!

THE THREE STOOGES #1
"Bed-Bugged!"

The Three Stooges

THE THREE STOOGES #2
"Ebenezer Stooge"

THE THREE STOOGES
BOING

THE BEST OF THE THREE STOOGES COMICBOOKS Vol. 1

THE THREE STOOGES

THE BEST OF THE THREE STOOGES COMICBOOKS Vol. 2

ANNOYING ORANGE, PAPERCUTZ SLICES and THE THREE STOOGES graphic novels, the print editions, are still available at booksellers everywhere.

ANNOYING ORANGE, PAPERCUTZ SLICES, and THE THREE STOOGES are available in paperback for $6.99 each; in hardcover for $10.99, except ANNOYING ORANGE #2, hardcover is $11.99, and ANNOYING ORANGE #3, #4, and #5 are $7.99 paperback, and $11.99 hardcover. THE BEST OF THE THREE STOOGES COMICBOOKS are available only in hardcover for $19.99 each. Please add $4.00 for postage and handling for the first book, and add $1.00 for each additional book. Make check payable to NBM Publishing.

Send to: Papercutz, 160 Broadway, Suite 700, East Wing, New York, NY 10038

Or call 800 886 1223 (9-6 EST M-F) MC-Visa-Amex accepted

papercutz.com

ANNOYING ORANGE and PAPERCUTZ SLICES graphic novels are also available digitally wherever e-books are sold.

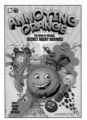

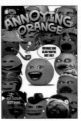

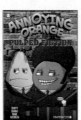

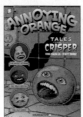

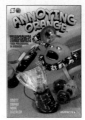

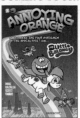

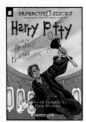

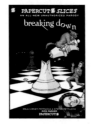

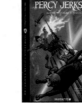

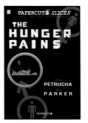

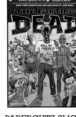

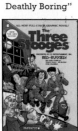

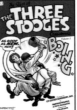

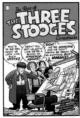

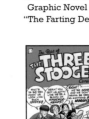

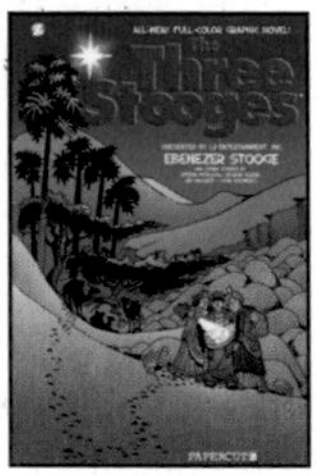

ANNOYING ORANGE™

TRANSFARMERS

FOOD PROCESSORS IN DISGUISE!

I THOUGHT THEY WERE GOING TO USE ME MORE IN THIS *GRAPHIC NOVEL,* BUT I GUESS I DIDN'T MAKE THE *CUT!*

WITHDRAWN

Annoying Orange is created by DANE BOEDIGHEIMER

SCOTT SHAW! – Writer & Artist

MIKE KAZALEH – Writer & Artist

LAURIE E. SMITH – Colorist

PAPERCUTZ™
NEW YORK

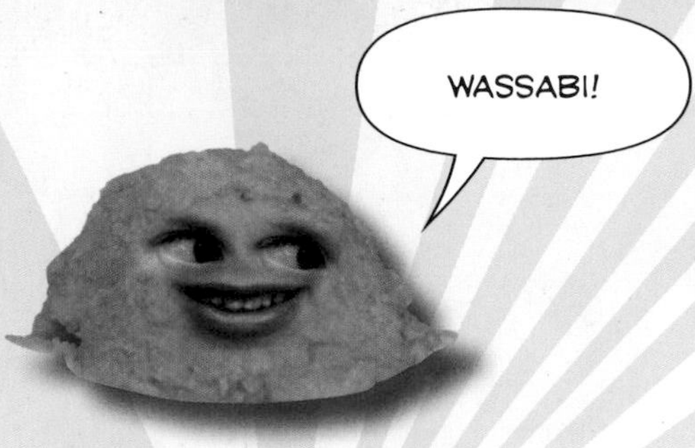
WASSABI!

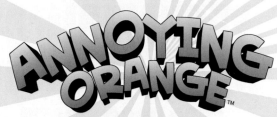

ANNOYING ORANGE™

 # 5 "Transfarmers: Food Processors in Disguise"

"The Amazing... Apple?" "Orange Tries a New Hobby" "Nightmare Pear" "A Sticky Situation"
"Passion Fruit Diaries" "Ask Orange" "The Adventures of the Coconut Custard Pie"
"I Was a 1 ½ Gram Softie" "Gratitude" "An Offer You Can't Refuse"

Mike Kazaleh – Writer & Artist
Laurie E. Smith – Colorist
Chris Nelson – Letterer

"Attack of the Tranfarmers: Food Processors in Disguise!"

Scott Shaw! – Writer & Artist
Laurie E. Smith – Colorist
Chris Nelson – Letterer
Christian Zanier – Cover Artist

Special thanks to:Gary Binkow, Tim Blankley, Dane Boedigheimer,
Spencer Grove, Teresa Harris, Reza Izad, Debra Joester, Polina Rey, Tom Sheppard
Production Coordinator: Beth Scorzato
Associate Editor: Michael Petranek
Jim Salicrup
Editor-in-Chief

ISBN: 978-1-59707-502-2 paperback edition
ISBN: 978-1-59707-503-9 hardcover edition

Printed in the US
April 2014 by Bang Printing
3323 Oak Street
Brainerd, MN 56401

Distributed by Macmillan
First Printing

MEET THE FRUIT...

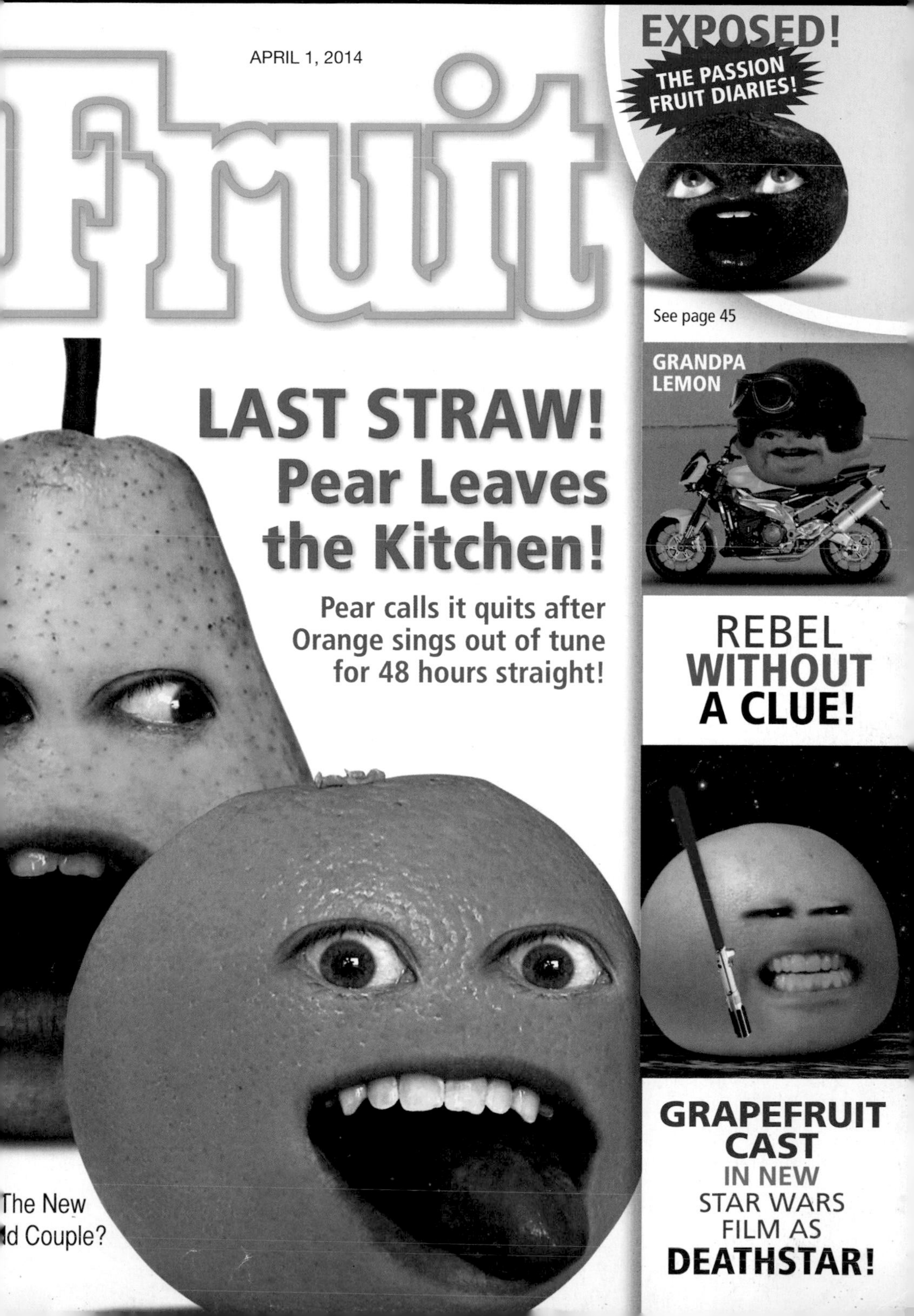
APRIL 1, 2014
Fruit
EXPOSED!
THE PASSION FRUIT DIARIES!
See page 45
LAST STRAW! Pear Leaves the Kitchen!
Pear calls it quits after Orange sings out of tune for 48 hours straight!
GRANDPA LEMON
REBEL WITHOUT A CLUE!
GRAPEFRUIT CAST IN NEW STAR WARS FILM AS DEATHSTAR!
The New
d Couple?

TV & Web Stars
GET GRAPHIC NOVEL MAKEOVERS

ORANGE

"Hey, look!
I'm a cartoon!"
The ever-annoying
Orange proves that
Orange is the
new Blechh!

PEAR

Orange's BFF poses
the query, "What's
a Kazaleh? Some
kind of mellon?"

**GRANDPA
LEMON**

Offers a typical
dazed and
confused response,
"I'm not Shaw!"

**MIDGET
APPLE**

"The artists for the
comics are great—
except they keep
drawing me
too small!"

BEST UNDRESSED

PASSION FRUIT

"Oh, I simply adore how they draw me! It's cool being a cartoon!"

APPLE

"Gee, it only took them five graphic novels before they included me in the 'Meet the Fruit...'"

MARSH- MALLOW

"That's funny, Apple! I'm in the 'Meet the Fruit...' pages and I'm not even a fruit!"

GRAPEFRUIT

"No one knows what you are, Marshmallow, and you're just being an apple, Apple!"

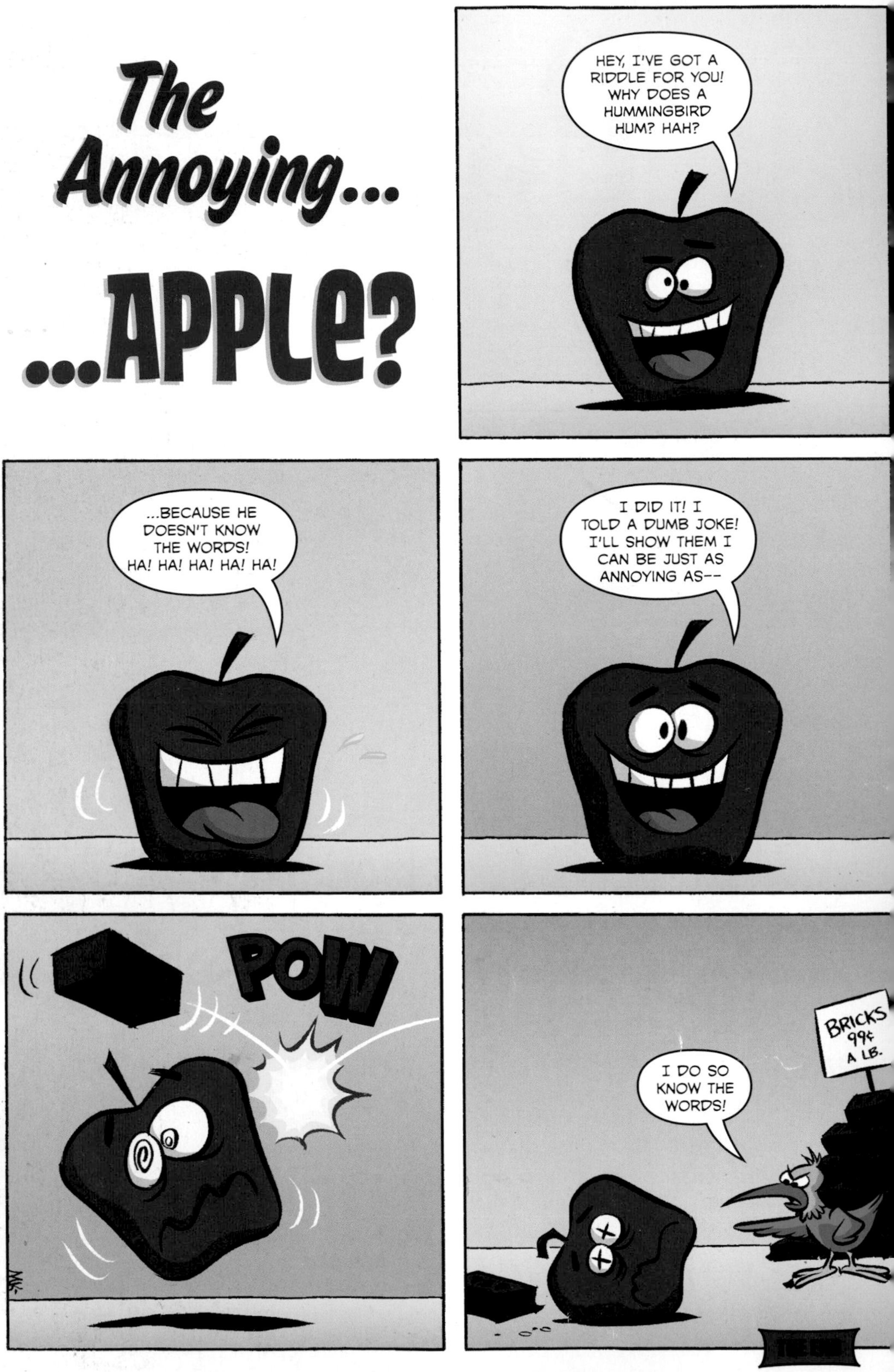
The Annoying...
...APPLE?
HEY, I'VE GOT A RIDDLE FOR YOU! WHY DOES A HUMMINGBIRD HUM? HAH?
...BECAUSE HE DOESN'T KNOW THE WORDS! HA! HA! HA! HA! HA!
I DID IT! I TOLD A DUMB JOKE! I'LL SHOW THEM I CAN BE JUST AS ANNOYING AS--
POW
BRICKS 99¢ A LB.
I DO SO KNOW THE WORDS!

ORANGE TRIES A NEW HOBBY

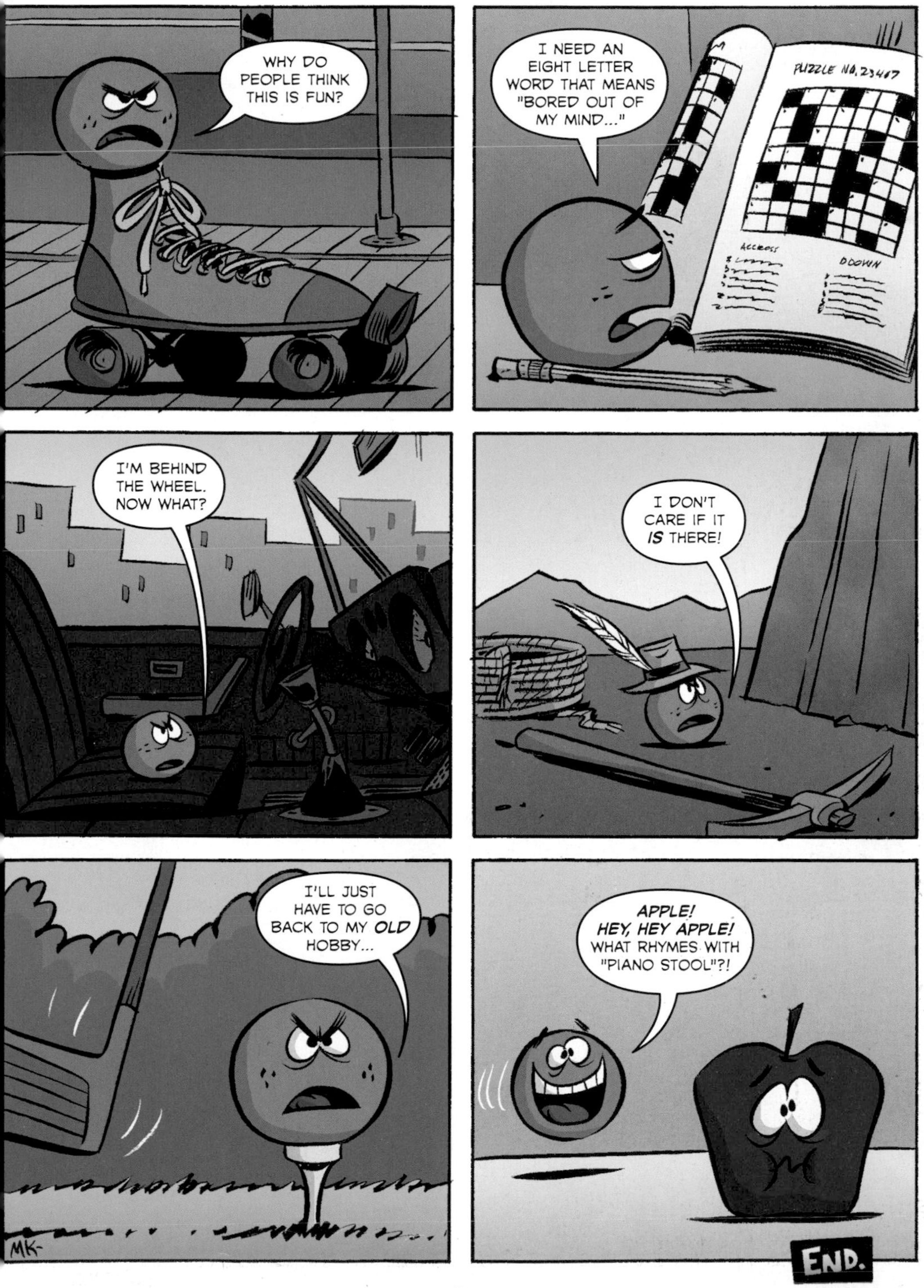

WHY DO PEOPLE THINK THIS IS FUN?
I NEED AN EIGHT LETTER WORD THAT MEANS "BORED OUT OF MY MIND..."
PUZZLE NO. 23467
I'M BEHIND THE WHEEL. NOW WHAT?
I DON'T CARE IF IT *IS* THERE!
I'LL JUST HAVE TO GO BACK TO MY *OLD* HOBBY...
MK
APPLE!
HEY, HEY APPLE!
WHAT RHYMES WITH "PIANO STOOL"?!
END.

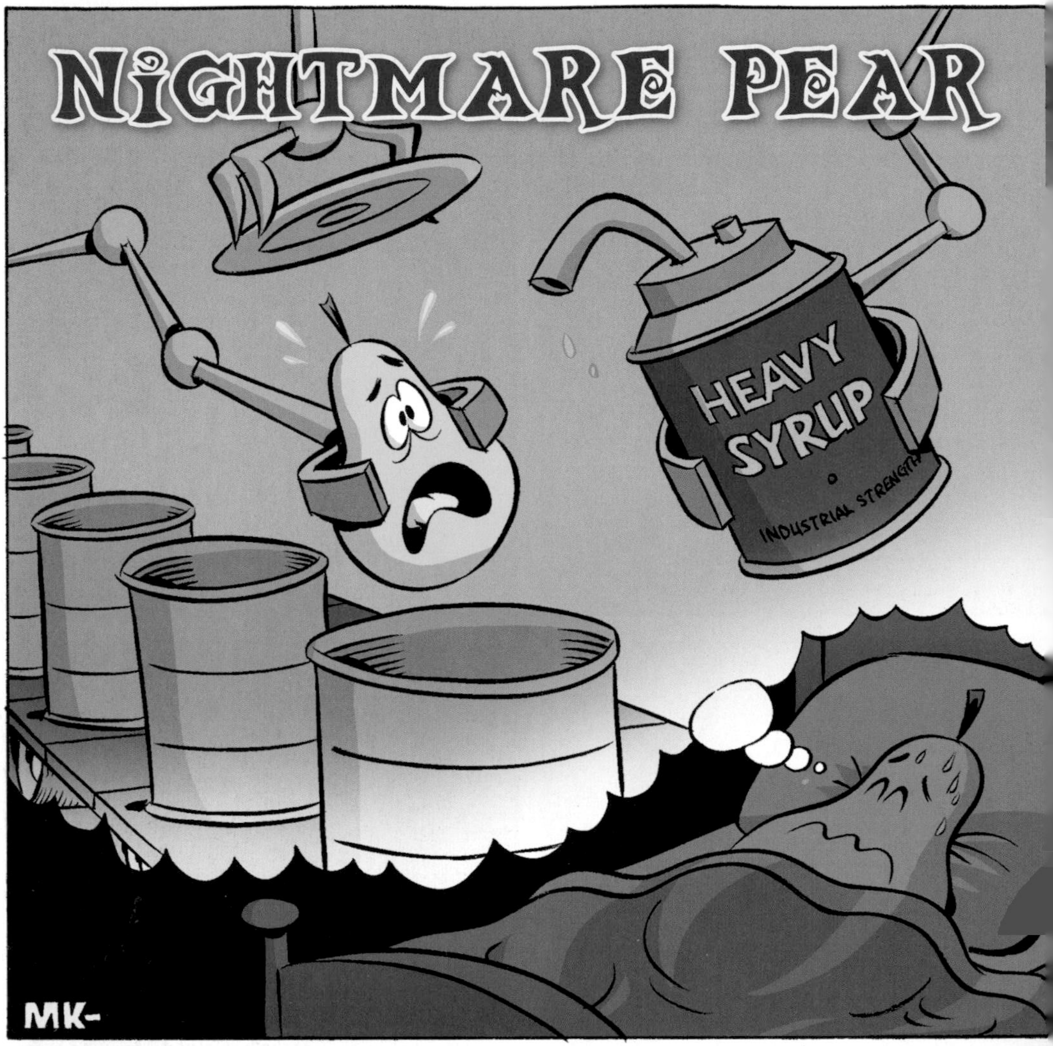
NIGHTMARE PEAR
HEAVY SYRUP
INDUSTRIAL STRENGTH
MK-

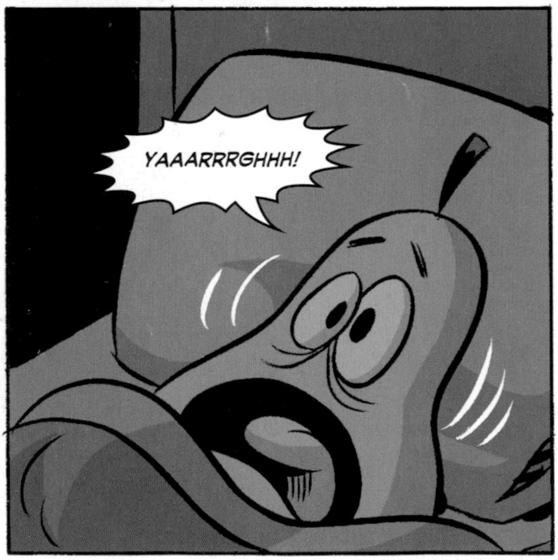
YAAARRRGHHH!

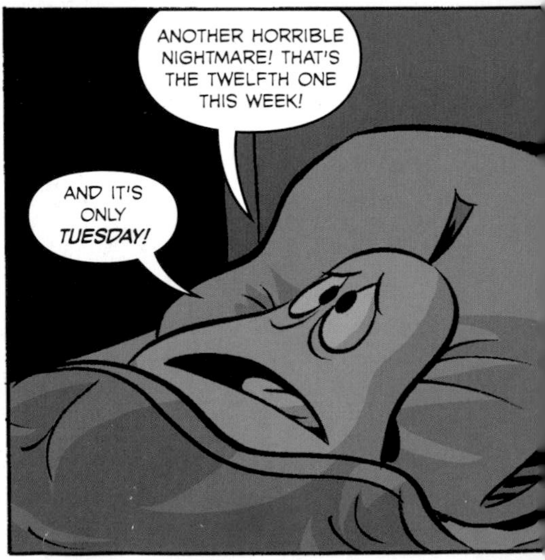
ANOTHER HORRIBLE NIGHTMARE! THAT'S THE TWELFTH ONE THIS WEEK!
AND IT'S ONLY TUESDAY!

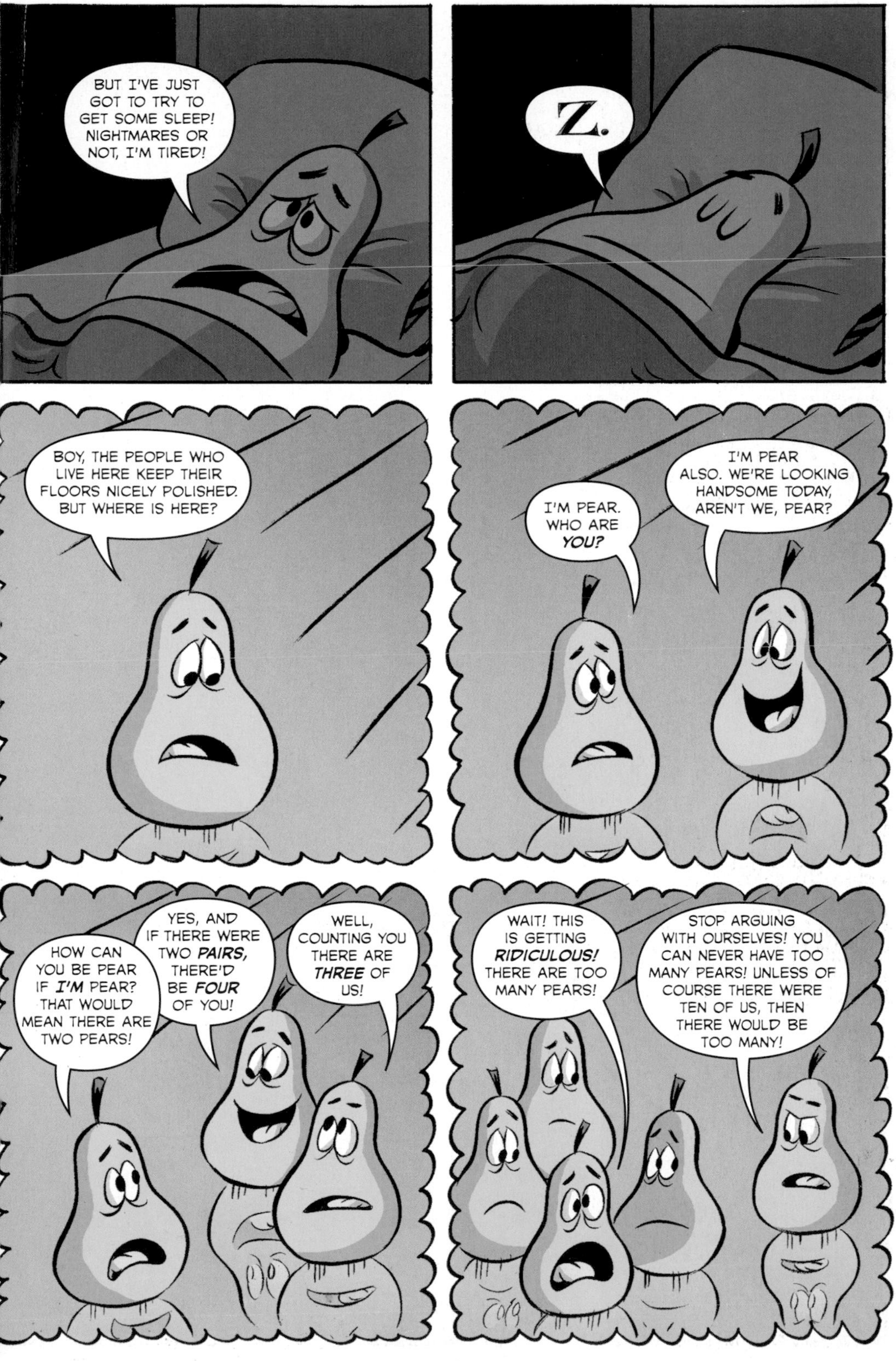
BUT I'VE JUST GOT TO TRY TO GET SOME SLEEP! NIGHTMARES OR NOT, I'M TIRED!
Z.
BOY, THE PEOPLE WHO LIVE HERE KEEP THEIR FLOORS NICELY POLISHED. BUT WHERE IS HERE?
I'M PEAR. WHO ARE YOU?
I'M PEAR ALSO. WE'RE LOOKING HANDSOME TODAY, AREN'T WE, PEAR?
HOW CAN YOU BE PEAR IF I'M PEAR? THAT WOULD MEAN THERE ARE TWO PEARS!
YES, AND IF THERE WERE TWO PAIRS, THERE'D BE FOUR OF YOU!
WELL, COUNTING YOU THERE ARE THREE OF US!
WAIT! THIS IS GETTING RIDICULOUS! THERE ARE TOO MANY PEARS!
STOP ARGUING WITH OURSELVES! YOU CAN NEVER HAVE TOO MANY PEARS! UNLESS OF COURSE THERE WERE TEN OF US, THEN THERE WOULD BE TOO MANY!

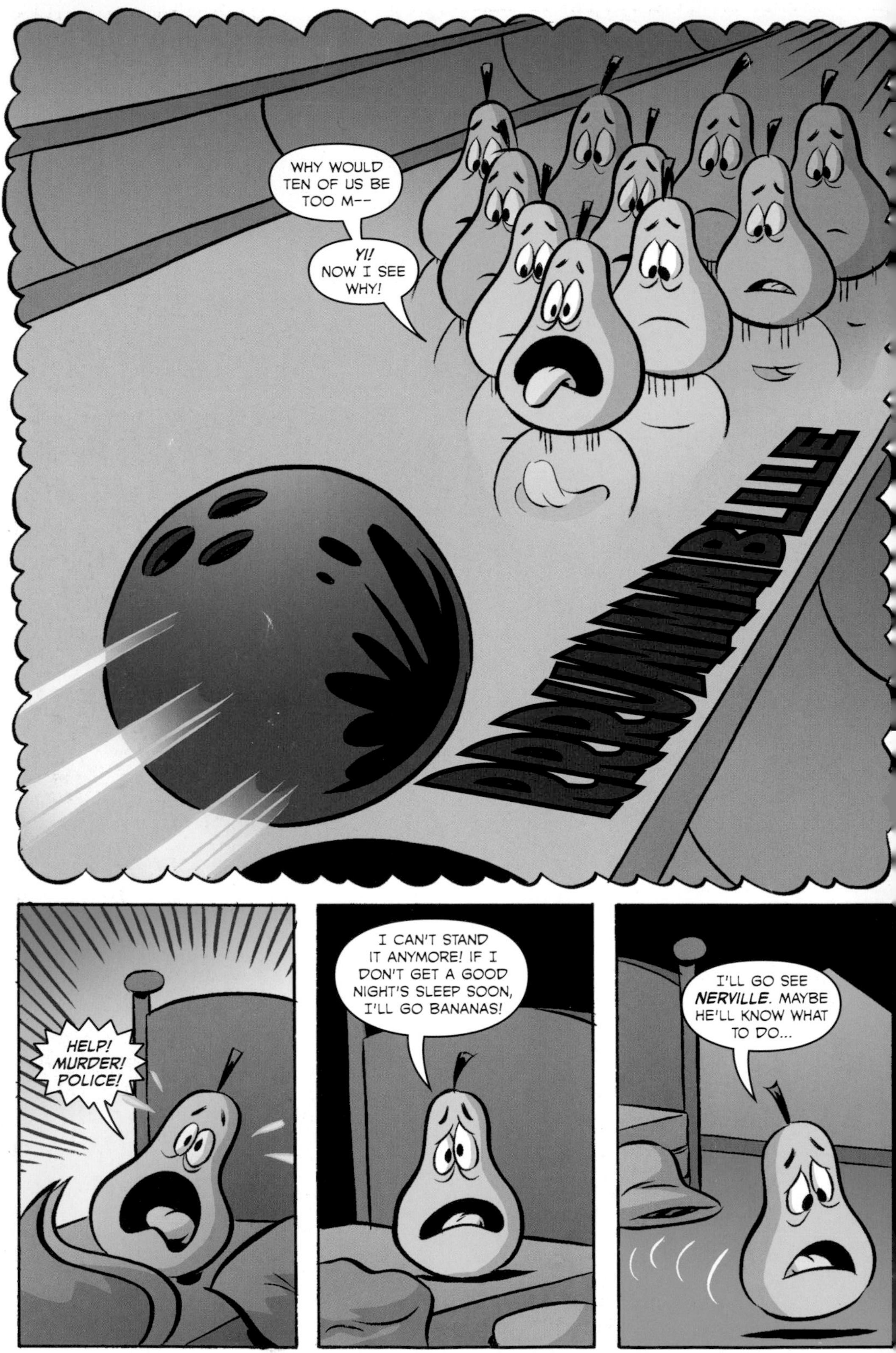
WHY WOULD TEN OF US BE TOO M--
YI! NOW I SEE WHY!
BRRRUMMMBLLLE
HELP! MURDER! POLICE!
I CAN'T STAND IT ANYMORE! IF I DON'T GET A GOOD NIGHT'S SLEEP SOON, I'LL GO BANANAS!
I'LL GO SEE NERVILLE. MAYBE HE'LL KNOW WHAT TO DO...

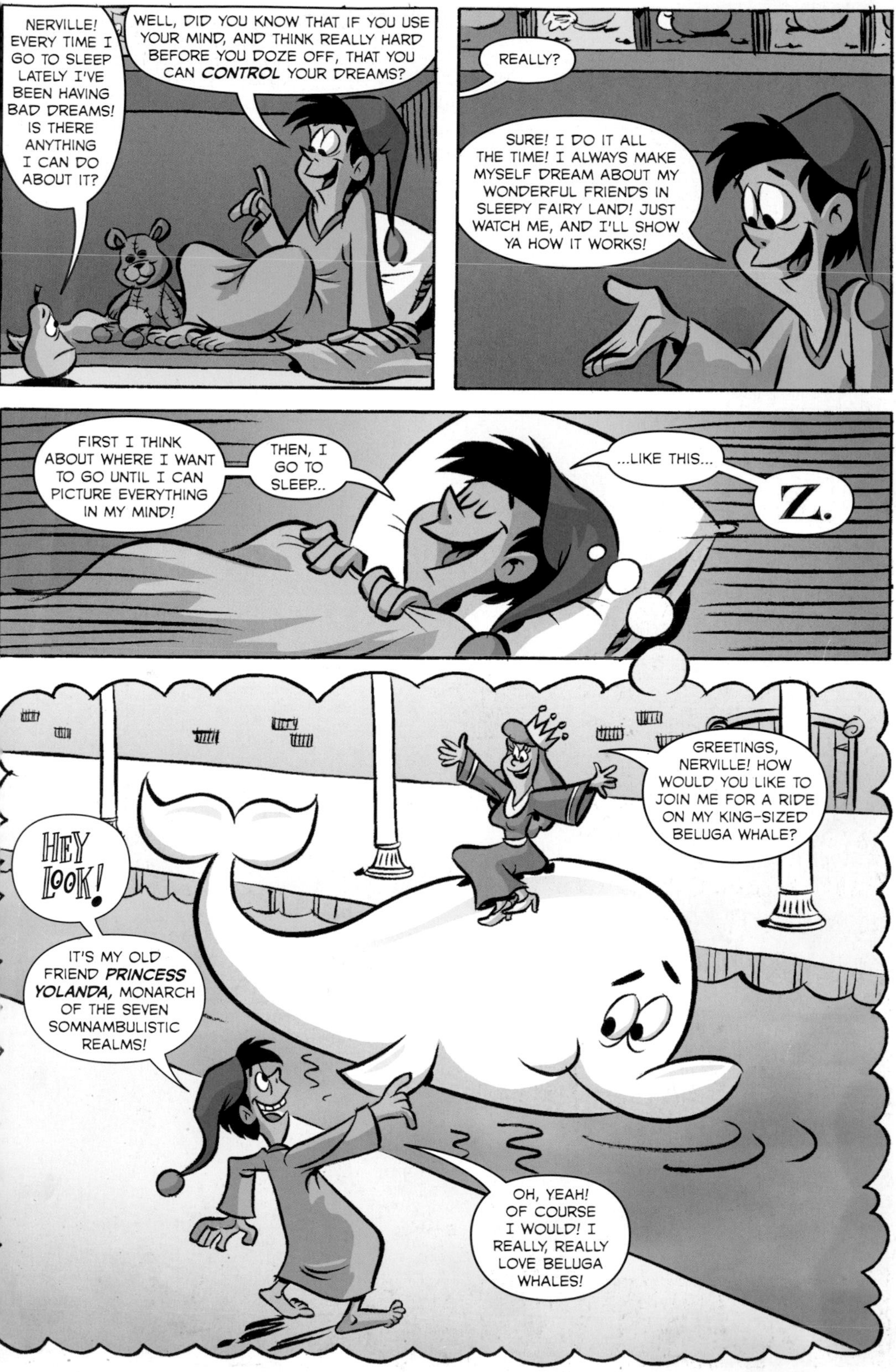
NERVILLE! EVERY TIME I GO TO SLEEP LATELY I'VE BEEN HAVING BAD DREAMS! IS THERE ANYTHING I CAN DO ABOUT IT?
WELL, DID YOU KNOW THAT IF YOU USE YOUR MIND, AND THINK REALLY HARD BEFORE YOU DOZE OFF, THAT YOU CAN **CONTROL** YOUR DREAMS?
REALLY?
SURE! I DO IT ALL THE TIME! I ALWAYS MAKE MYSELF DREAM ABOUT MY WONDERFUL FRIENDS IN SLEEPY FAIRY LAND! JUST WATCH ME, AND I'LL SHOW YA HOW IT WORKS!
FIRST I THINK ABOUT WHERE I WANT TO GO UNTIL I CAN PICTURE EVERYTHING IN MY MIND!
THEN, I GO TO SLEEP...
...LIKE THIS...
Z.
GREETINGS, NERVILLE! HOW WOULD YOU LIKE TO JOIN ME FOR A RIDE ON MY KING-SIZED BELUGA WHALE?
HEY LOOK!
IT'S MY OLD FRIEND **PRINCESS YOLANDA,** MONARCH OF THE SEVEN SOMNAMBULISTIC REALMS!
OH, YEAH! OF COURSE I WOULD! I REALLY, REALLY LOVE BELUGA WHALES!

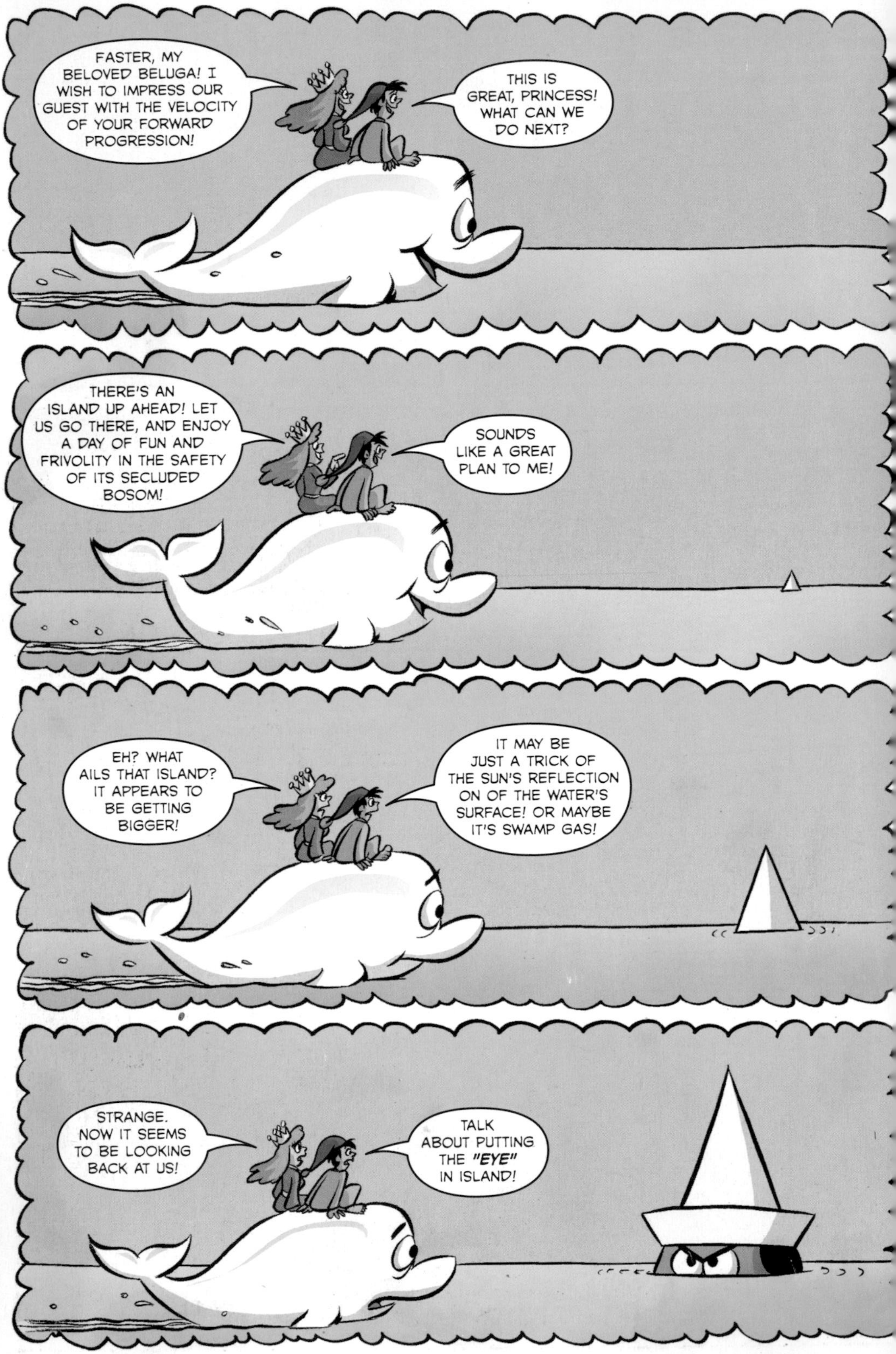
FASTER, MY BELOVED BELUGA! I WISH TO IMPRESS OUR GUEST WITH THE VELOCITY OF YOUR FORWARD PROGRESSION!
THIS IS GREAT, PRINCESS! WHAT CAN WE DO NEXT?
THERE'S AN ISLAND UP AHEAD! LET US GO THERE, AND ENJOY A DAY OF FUN AND FRIVOLITY IN THE SAFETY OF ITS SECLUDED BOSOM!
SOUNDS LIKE A GREAT PLAN TO ME!
EH? WHAT AILS THAT ISLAND? IT APPEARS TO BE GETTING BIGGER!
IT MAY BE JUST A TRICK OF THE SUN'S REFLECTION ON OF THE WATER'S SURFACE! OR MAYBE IT'S SWAMP GAS!
STRANGE. NOW IT SEEMS TO BE LOOKING BACK AT US!
TALK ABOUT PUTTING THE "EYE" IN ISLAND!

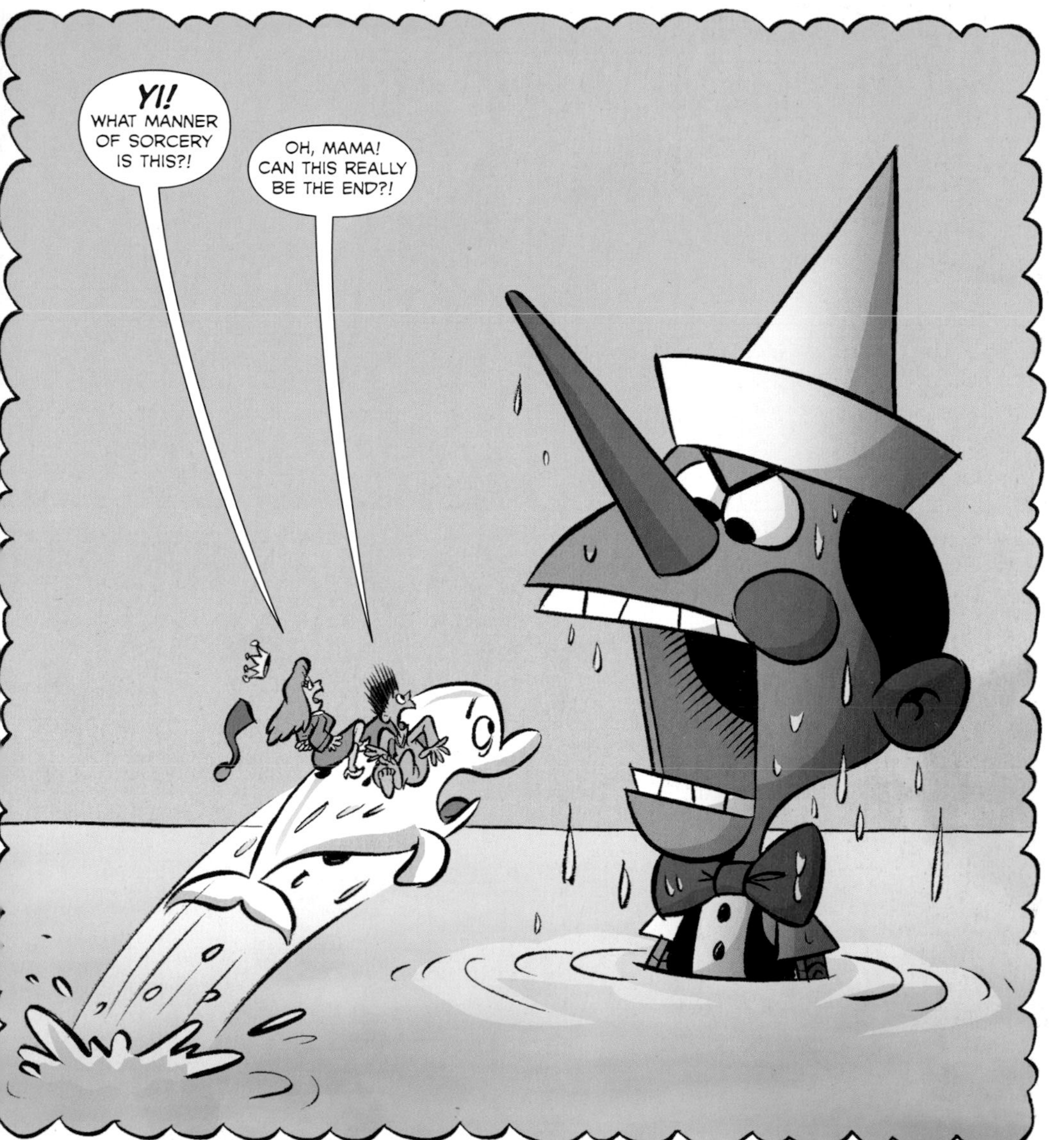
YI! WHAT MANNER OF SORCERY IS THIS?!
OH, MAMA! CAN THIS REALLY BE THE END?!

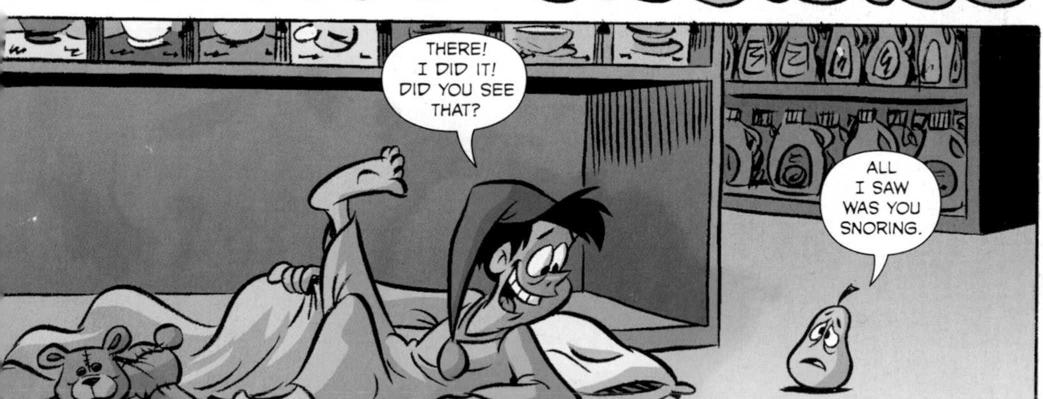
THERE! I DID IT! DID YOU SEE THAT?
ALL I SAW WAS YOU SNORING.

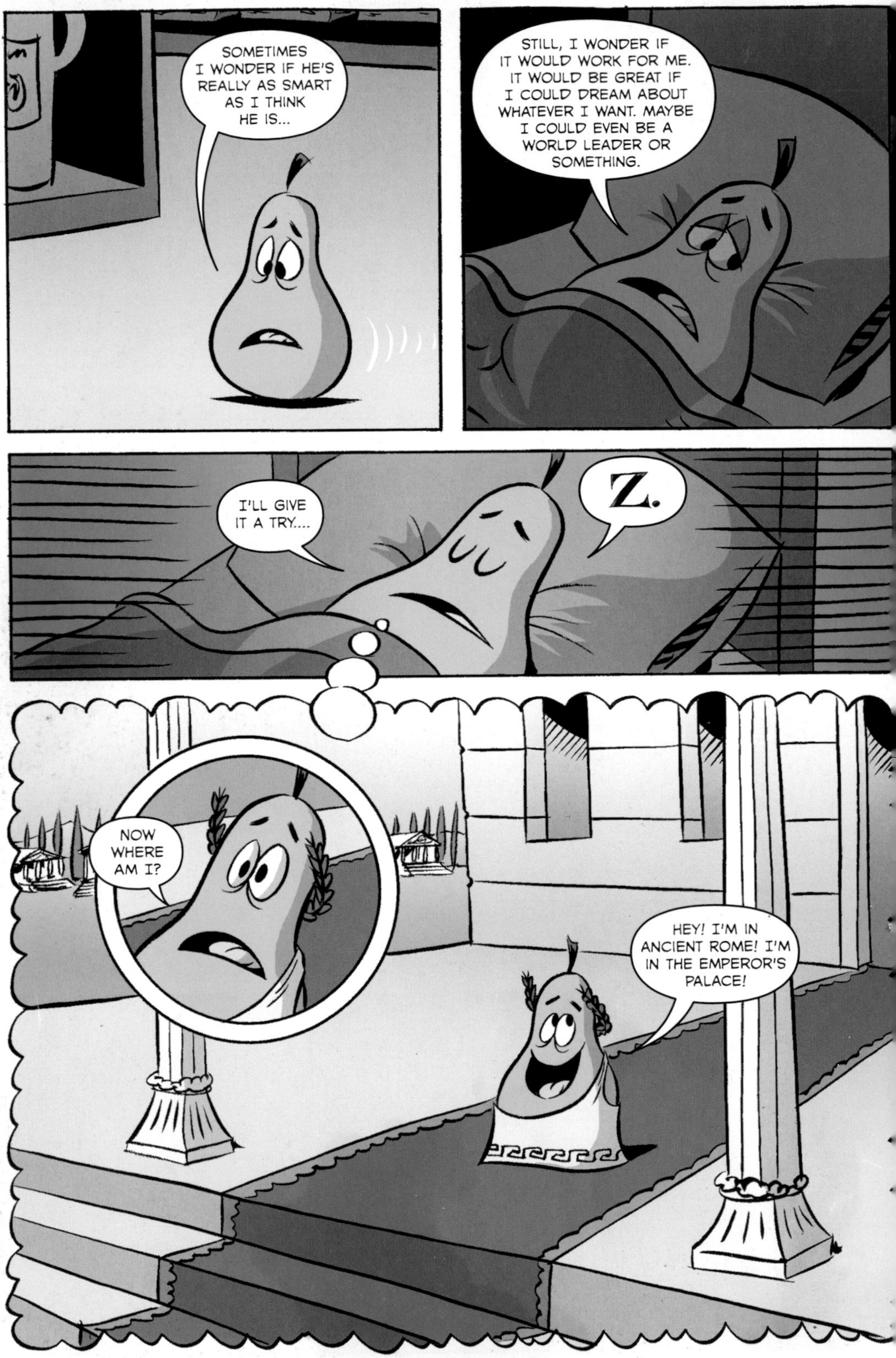
SOMETIMES I WONDER IF HE'S REALLY AS SMART AS I THINK HE IS...
STILL, I WONDER IF IT WOULD WORK FOR ME. IT WOULD BE GREAT IF I COULD DREAM ABOUT WHATEVER I WANT. MAYBE I COULD EVEN BE A WORLD LEADER OR SOMETHING.
I'LL GIVE IT A TRY....
Z.
NOW WHERE AM I?
HEY! I'M IN ANCIENT ROME! I'M IN THE EMPEROR'S PALACE!

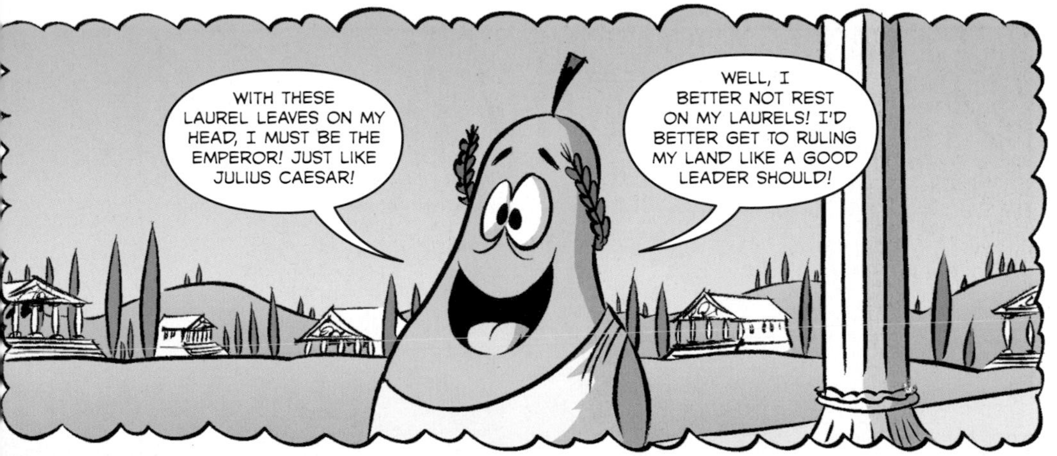
WITH THESE LAUREL LEAVES ON MY HEAD, I MUST BE THE EMPEROR! JUST LIKE JULIUS CAESAR!
WELL, I BETTER NOT REST ON MY LAURELS! I'D BETTER GET TO RULING MY LAND LIKE A GOOD LEADER SHOULD!

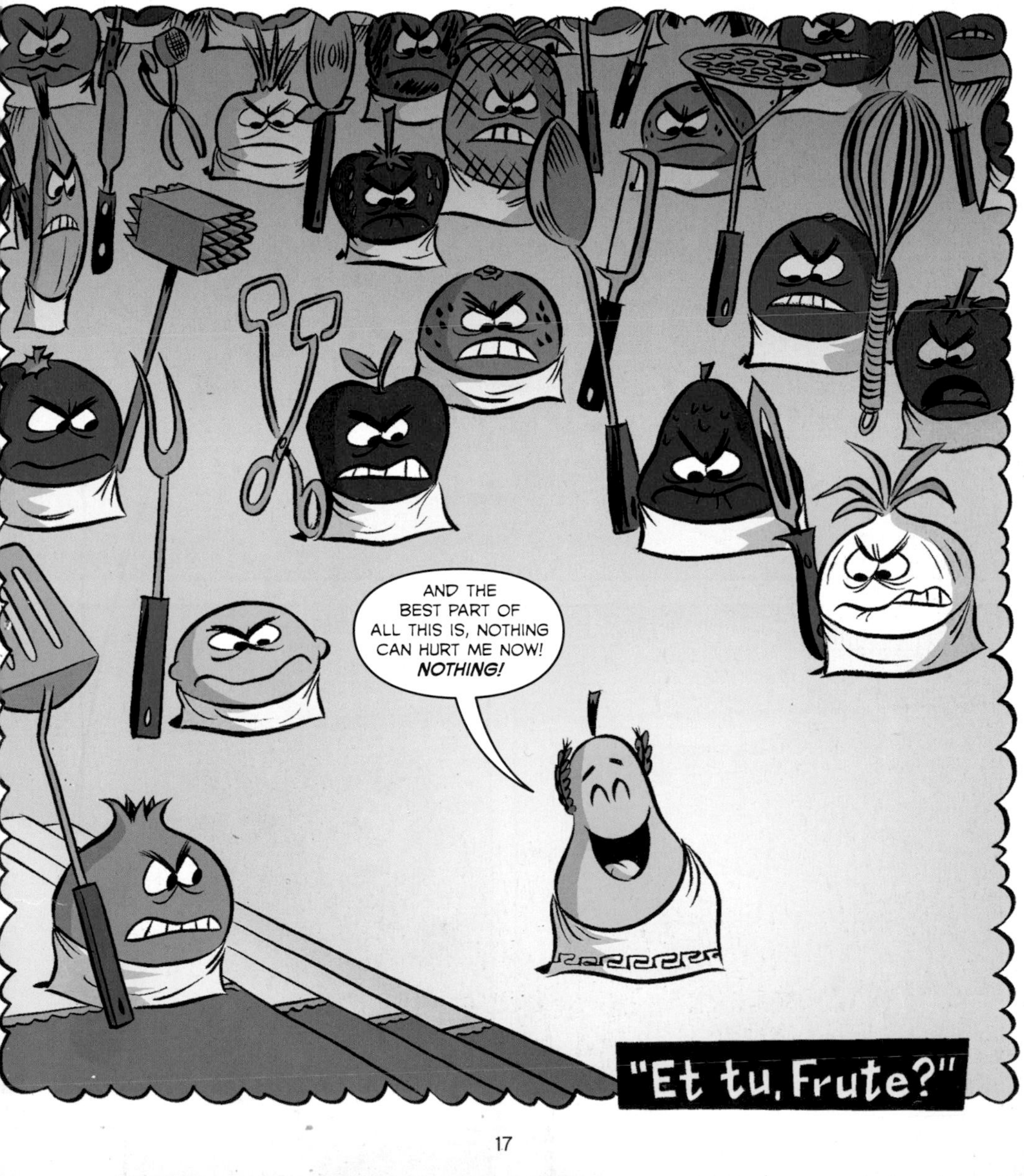
AND THE BEST PART OF ALL THIS IS, NOTHING CAN HURT ME NOW! ***NOTHING!***
"Et tu, Frute?"

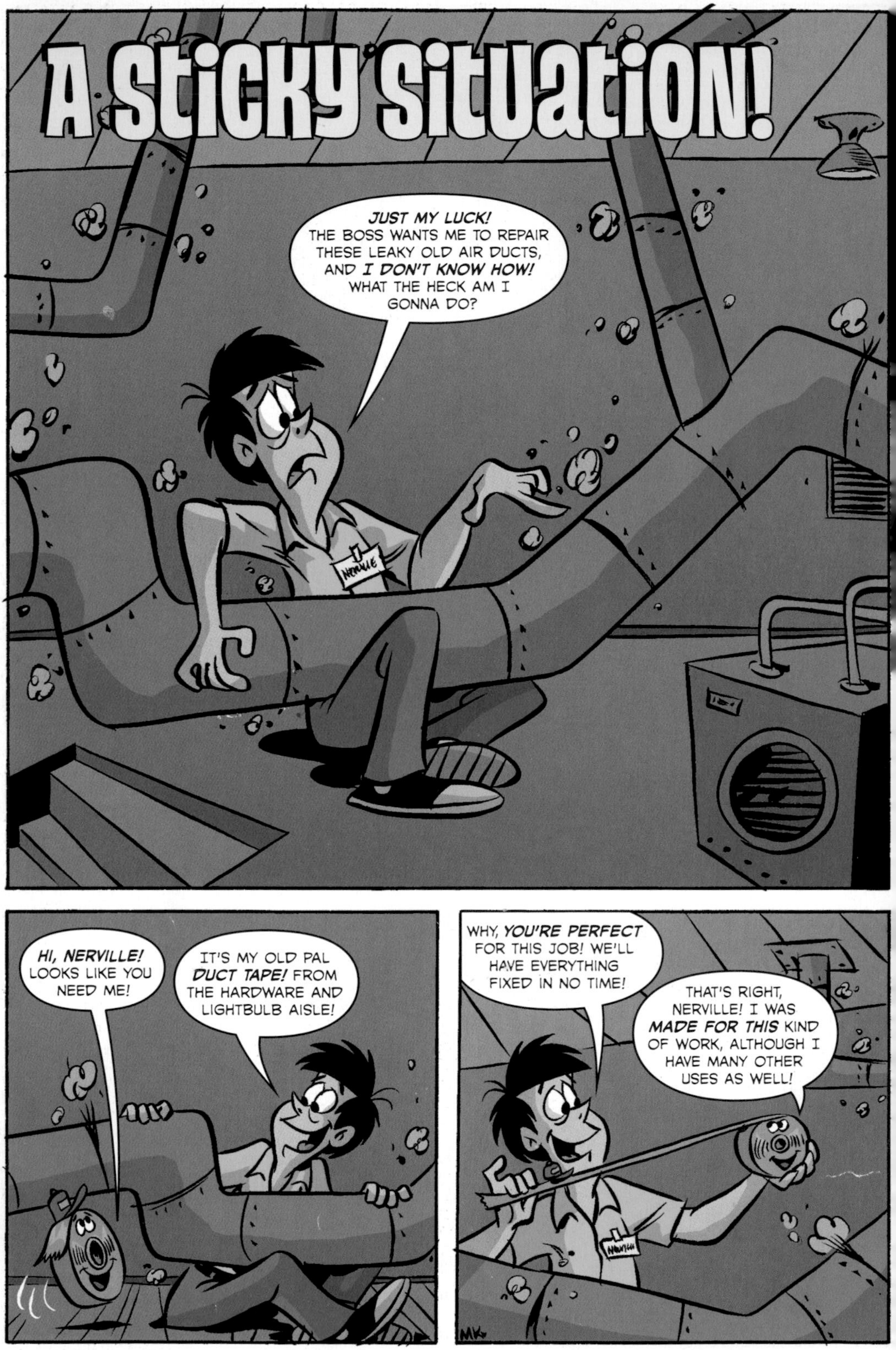
A STICKY SITUATION!
JUST MY LUCK! THE BOSS WANTS ME TO REPAIR THESE LEAKY OLD AIR DUCTS, AND I DON'T KNOW HOW! WHAT THE HECK AM I GONNA DO?
HI, NERVILLE! LOOKS LIKE YOU NEED ME!
IT'S MY OLD PAL DUCT TAPE! FROM THE HARDWARE AND LIGHTBULB AISLE!
WHY, YOU'RE PERFECT FOR THIS JOB! WE'LL HAVE EVERYTHING FIXED IN NO TIME!
THAT'S RIGHT, NERVILLE! I WAS MADE FOR THIS KIND OF WORK, ALTHOUGH I HAVE MANY OTHER USES AS WELL!

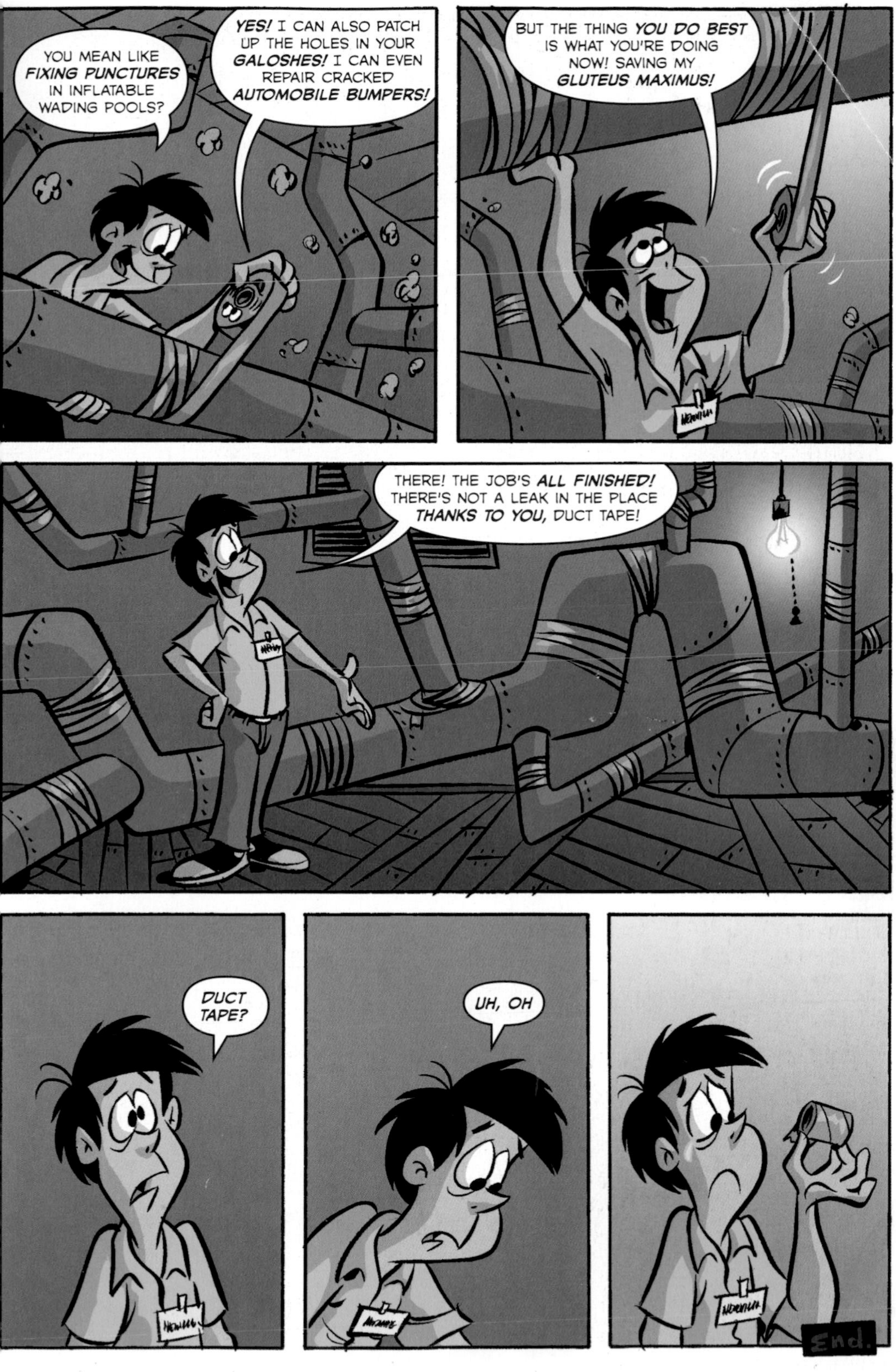
YOU MEAN LIKE FIXING PUNCTURES IN INFLATABLE WADING POOLS?
YES! I CAN ALSO PATCH UP THE HOLES IN YOUR GALOSHES! I CAN EVEN REPAIR CRACKED AUTOMOBILE BUMPERS!
BUT THE THING YOU DO BEST IS WHAT YOU'RE DOING NOW! SAVING MY GLUTEUS MAXIMUS!
THERE! THE JOB'S ALL FINISHED! THERE'S NOT A LEAK IN THE PLACE THANKS TO YOU, DUCT TAPE!
DUCT TAPE?
UH, OH
End.

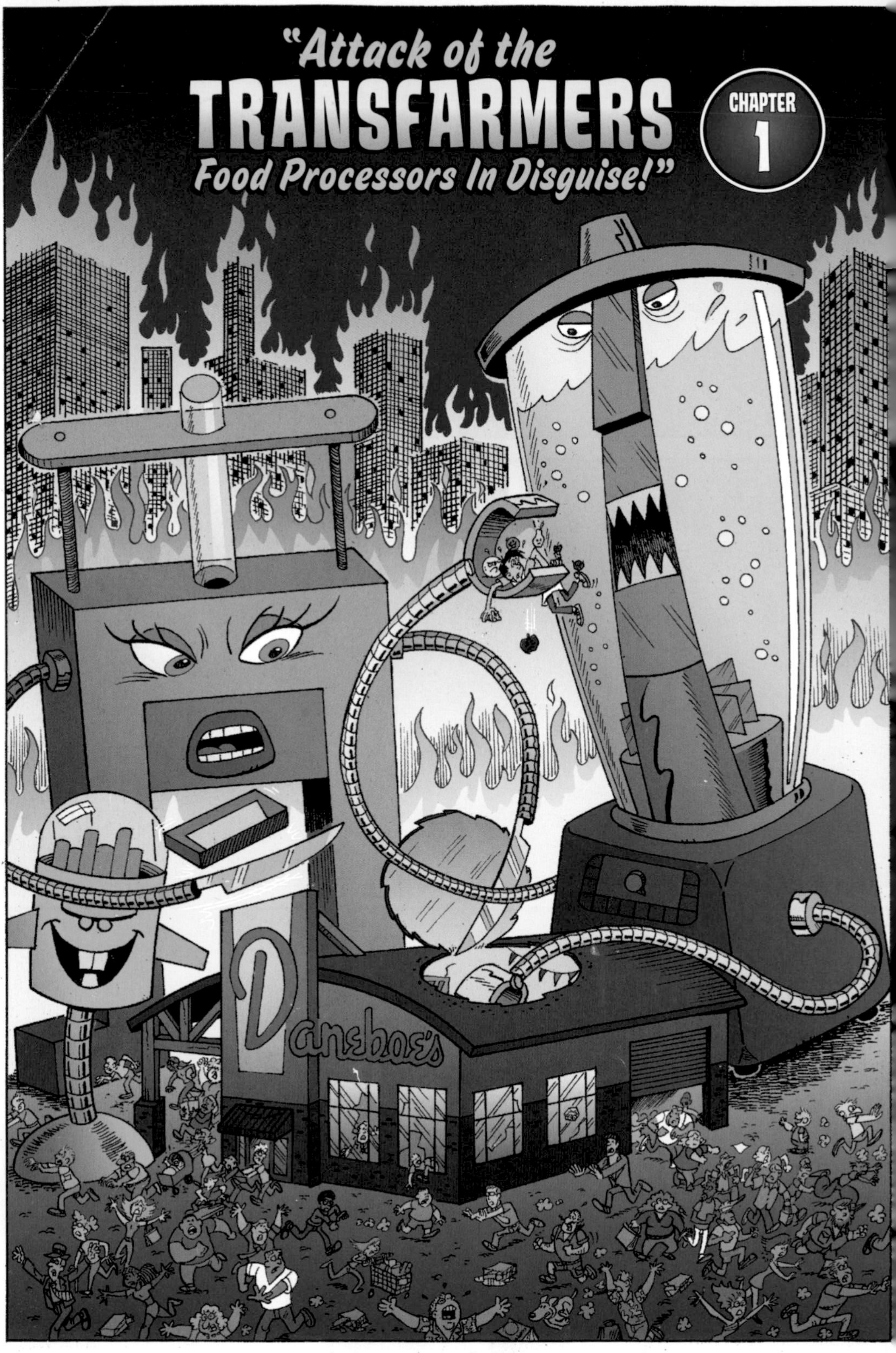
"Attack of the
TRANSFARMERS
Food Processors In Disguise!"
CHAPTER
1
Danshoe's

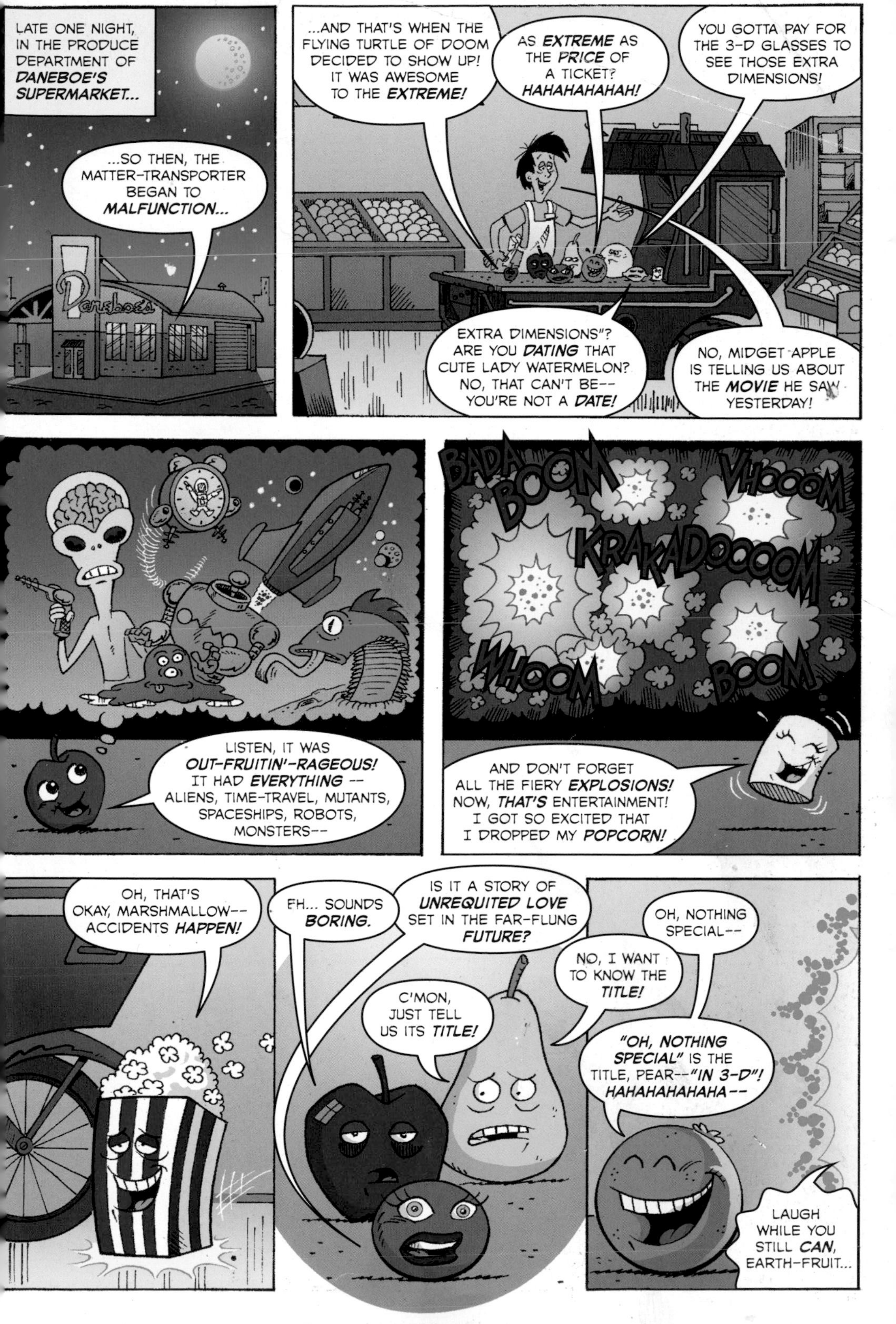

LATE ONE NIGHT, IN THE PRODUCE DEPARTMENT OF ***DANEBOE'S SUPERMARKET...***
...SO THEN, THE MATTER-TRANSPORTER BEGAN TO ***MALFUNCTION...***
Daneboe's
...AND THAT'S WHEN THE FLYING TURTLE OF DOOM DECIDED TO SHOW UP! IT WAS AWESOME TO THE ***EXTREME!***
AS ***EXTREME*** AS THE ***PRICE*** OF A TICKET? ***HAHAHAHAHAH!***
YOU GOTTA PAY FOR THE 3-D GLASSES TO SEE THOSE EXTRA DIMENSIONS!
EXTRA DIMENSIONS"? ARE YOU ***DATING*** THAT CUTE LADY WATERMELON? NO, THAT CAN'T BE-- YOU'RE NOT A ***DATE!***
NO, MIDGET APPLE IS TELLING US ABOUT THE ***MOVIE*** HE SAW YESTERDAY!
LISTEN, IT WAS ***OUT-FRUITIN'-RAGEOUS!*** IT HAD ***EVERYTHING*** -- ALIENS, TIME-TRAVEL, MUTANTS, SPACESHIPS, ROBOTS, MONSTERS--
BADA BOOM
VHOOOM
KRAKADOOOOM
WHOOM
BOOM
AND DON'T FORGET ALL THE FIERY ***EXPLOSIONS!*** NOW, ***THAT'S*** ENTERTAINMENT! I GOT SO EXCITED THAT I DROPPED MY ***POPCORN!***
OH, THAT'S OKAY, MARSHMALLOW-- ACCIDENTS ***HAPPEN!***
EH... SOUNDS ***BORING.***
IS IT A STORY OF ***UNREQUITED LOVE*** SET IN THE FAR-FLUNG ***FUTURE?***
C'MON, JUST TELL US ITS ***TITLE!***
OH, NOTHING SPECIAL--
NO, I WANT TO KNOW THE ***TITLE!***
"OH, NOTHING SPECIAL" IS THE TITLE, PEAR--***"IN 3-D"! HAHAHAHAHAHA--***
LAUGH WHILE YOU STILL ***CAN,*** EARTH-FRUIT...

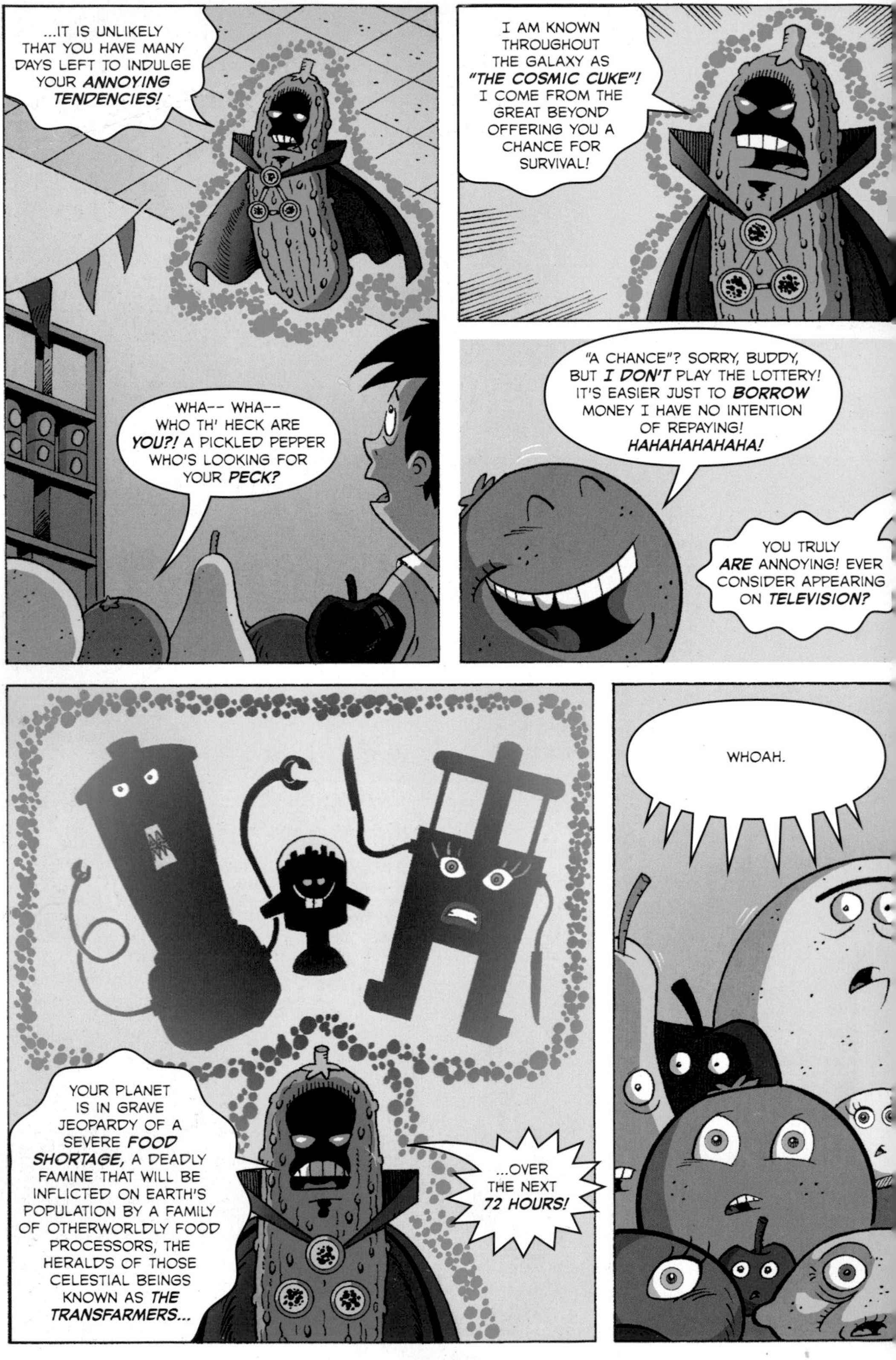
...IT IS UNLIKELY THAT YOU HAVE MANY DAYS LEFT TO INDULGE YOUR ANNOYING TENDENCIES!
WHA-- WHA-- WHO TH' HECK ARE YOU?! A PICKLED PEPPER WHO'S LOOKING FOR YOUR PECK?
I AM KNOWN THROUGHOUT THE GALAXY AS "THE COSMIC CUKE"! I COME FROM THE GREAT BEYOND OFFERING YOU A CHANCE FOR SURVIVAL!
"A CHANCE"? SORRY, BUDDY, BUT I DON'T PLAY THE LOTTERY! IT'S EASIER JUST TO BORROW MONEY I HAVE NO INTENTION OF REPAYING! HAHAHAHAHAHA!
YOU TRULY ARE ANNOYING! EVER CONSIDER APPEARING ON TELEVISION?
YOUR PLANET IS IN GRAVE JEOPARDY OF A SEVERE FOOD SHORTAGE, A DEADLY FAMINE THAT WILL BE INFLICTED ON EARTH'S POPULATION BY A FAMILY OF OTHERWORLDLY FOOD PROCESSORS, THE HERALDS OF THOSE CELESTIAL BEINGS KNOWN AS THE TRANSFARMERS...
...OVER THE NEXT 72 HOURS!
WHOAH.

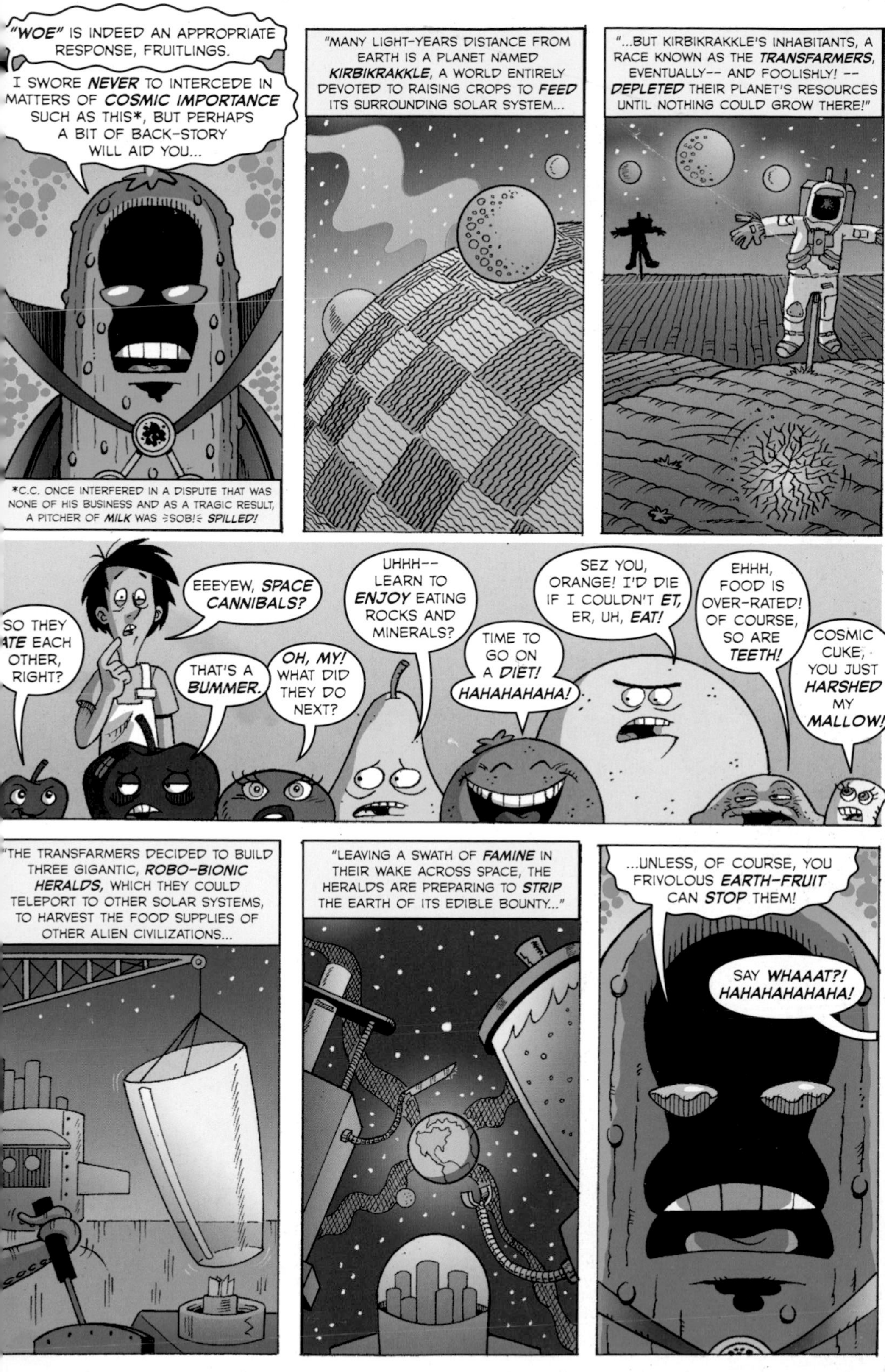
"WOE" IS INDEED AN APPROPRIATE RESPONSE, FRUITLINGS.
I SWORE NEVER TO INTERCEDE IN MATTERS OF COSMIC IMPORTANCE SUCH AS THIS*, BUT PERHAPS A BIT OF BACK-STORY WILL AID YOU...
*C.C. ONCE INTERFERED IN A DISPUTE THAT WAS NONE OF HIS BUSINESS AND AS A TRAGIC RESULT, A PITCHER OF MILK WAS >SOB!< SPILLED!
"MANY LIGHT-YEARS DISTANCE FROM EARTH IS A PLANET NAMED KIRBIKRAKKLE, A WORLD ENTIRELY DEVOTED TO RAISING CROPS TO FEED ITS SURROUNDING SOLAR SYSTEM...
"...BUT KIRBIKRAKKLE'S INHABITANTS, A RACE KNOWN AS THE TRANSFARMERS, EVENTUALLY-- AND FOOLISHLY! -- DEPLETED THEIR PLANET'S RESOURCES UNTIL NOTHING COULD GROW THERE!"
SO THEY ATE EACH OTHER, RIGHT?
EEEYEW, SPACE CANNIBALS?
THAT'S A BUMMER.
OH, MY! WHAT DID THEY DO NEXT?
UHHH-- LEARN TO ENJOY EATING ROCKS AND MINERALS?
TIME TO GO ON A DIET! HAHAHAHAHA!
SEZ YOU, ORANGE! I'D DIE IF I COULDN'T ET, ER, UH, EAT!
EHHH, FOOD IS OVER-RATED! OF COURSE, SO ARE TEETH!
COSMIC CUKE, YOU JUST HARSHED MY MALLOW!
"THE TRANSFARMERS DECIDED TO BUILD THREE GIGANTIC, ROBO-BIONIC HERALDS, WHICH THEY COULD TELEPORT TO OTHER SOLAR SYSTEMS, TO HARVEST THE FOOD SUPPLIES OF OTHER ALIEN CIVILIZATIONS...
"LEAVING A SWATH OF FAMINE IN THEIR WAKE ACROSS SPACE, THE HERALDS ARE PREPARING TO STRIP THE EARTH OF ITS EDIBLE BOUNTY..."
...UNLESS, OF COURSE, YOU FRIVOLOUS EARTH-FRUIT CAN STOP THEM!
SAY WHAAAT?! HAHAHAHAHAHA!

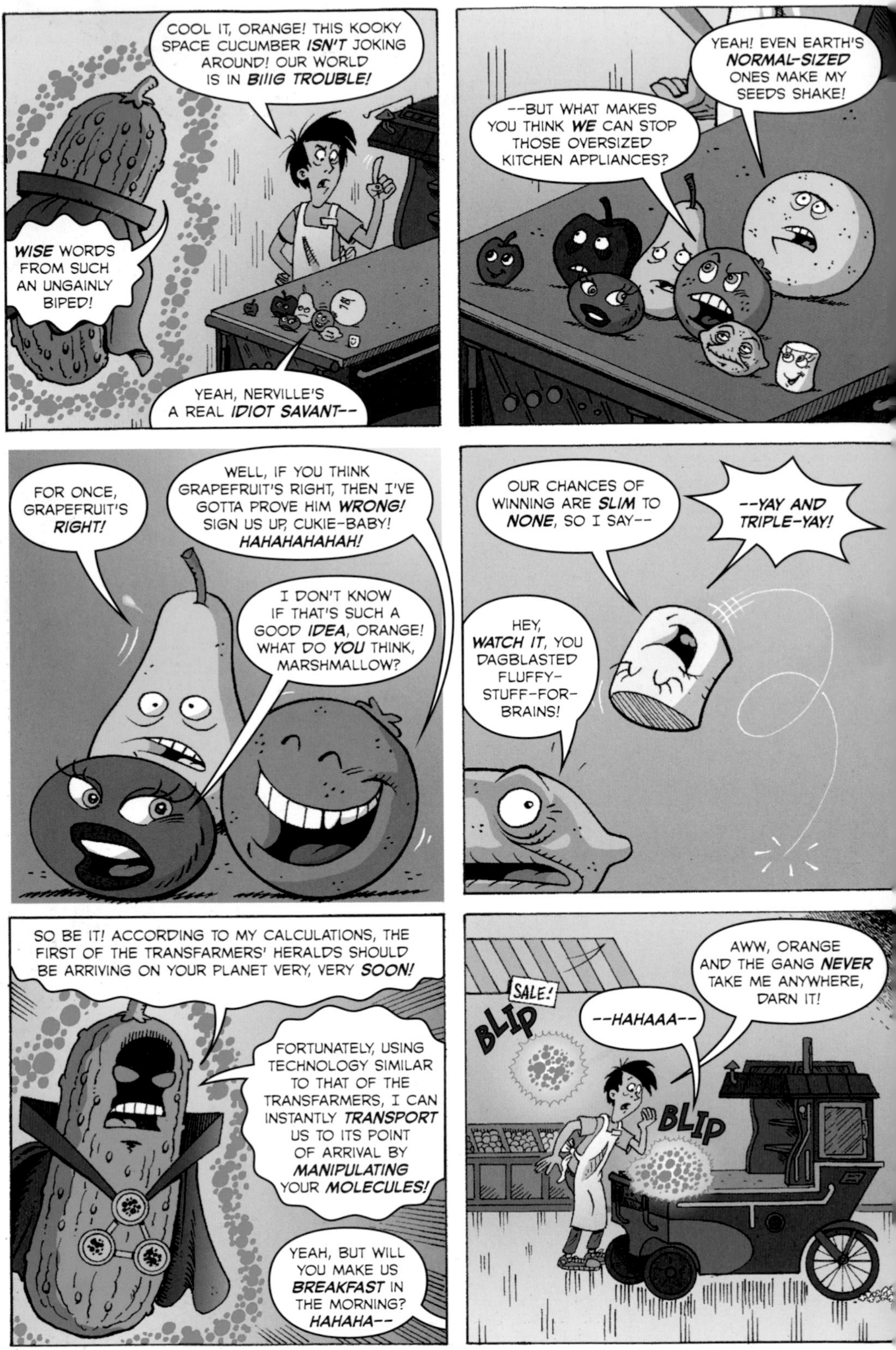
COOL IT, ORANGE! THIS KOOKY SPACE CUCUMBER ISN'T JOKING AROUND! OUR WORLD IS IN BIIIG TROUBLE!
WISE WORDS FROM SUCH AN UNGAINLY BIPED!
YEAH, NERVILLE'S A REAL IDIOT SAVANT--
--BUT WHAT MAKES YOU THINK WE CAN STOP THOSE OVERSIZED KITCHEN APPLIANCES?
YEAH! EVEN EARTH'S NORMAL-SIZED ONES MAKE MY SEEDS SHAKE!
FOR ONCE, GRAPEFRUIT'S RIGHT!
WELL, IF YOU THINK GRAPEFRUIT'S RIGHT, THEN I'VE GOTTA PROVE HIM WRONG! SIGN US UP, CUKIE-BABY! HAHAHAHAHAH!
I DON'T KNOW IF THAT'S SUCH A GOOD IDEA, ORANGE! WHAT DO YOU THINK, MARSHMALLOW?
OUR CHANCES OF WINNING ARE SLIM TO NONE, SO I SAY--
--YAY AND TRIPLE-YAY!
HEY, WATCH IT, YOU DAGBLASTED FLUFFY-STUFF-FOR-BRAINS!
SO BE IT! ACCORDING TO MY CALCULATIONS, THE FIRST OF THE TRANSFARMERS' HERALDS SHOULD BE ARRIVING ON YOUR PLANET VERY, VERY SOON!
FORTUNATELY, USING TECHNOLOGY SIMILAR TO THAT OF THE TRANSFARMERS, I CAN INSTANTLY TRANSPORT US TO ITS POINT OF ARRIVAL BY MANIPULATING YOUR MOLECULES!
YEAH, BUT WILL YOU MAKE US BREAKFAST IN THE MORNING? HAHAHA--
SALE!
BLIP
--HAHAAA--
AWW, ORANGE AND THE GANG NEVER TAKE ME ANYWHERE, DARN IT!
BLIP

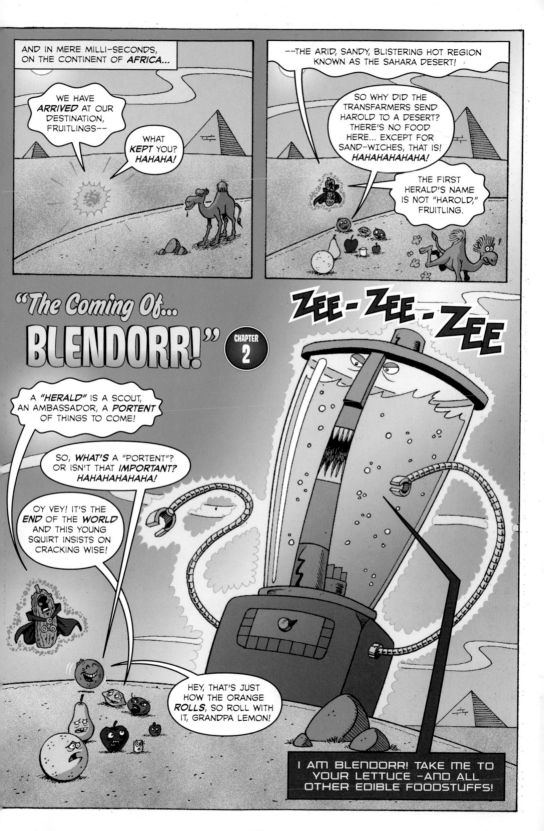

AND IN MERE MILLI-SECONDS, ON THE CONTINENT OF *AFRICA*...

WE HAVE *ARRIVED* AT OUR DESTINATION, FRUITLINGS--

WHAT *KEPT* YOU? HAHAHA!

--THE ARID, SANDY, BLISTERING HOT REGION KNOWN AS THE SAHARA DESERT!

SO WHY DID THE TRANSFARMERS SEND HAROLD TO A DESERT? THERE'S NO FOOD HERE... EXCEPT FOR SAND-WICHES, THAT IS! HAHAHAHAHAHA!

THE FIRST HERALD'S NAME IS NOT "HAROLD," FRUITLING.

"The Coming Of... BLENDORR!" CHAPTER 2

ZEE-ZEE-ZEE

A *"HERALD"* IS A SCOUT, AN AMBASSADOR, A *PORTENT* OF THINGS TO COME!

SO, *WHAT'S* A "PORTENT"? OR ISN'T THAT *IMPORTANT*? HAHAHAHAHAHA!

OY VEY! IT'S THE *END* OF THE *WORLD* AND THIS YOUNG SQUIRT INSISTS ON CRACKING WISE!

HEY, THAT'S JUST HOW THE ORANGE *ROLLS*, SO ROLL WITH IT, GRANDPA LEMON!

I AM BLENDORR! TAKE ME TO YOUR LETTUCE -AND ALL OTHER EDIBLE FOODSTUFFS!

25

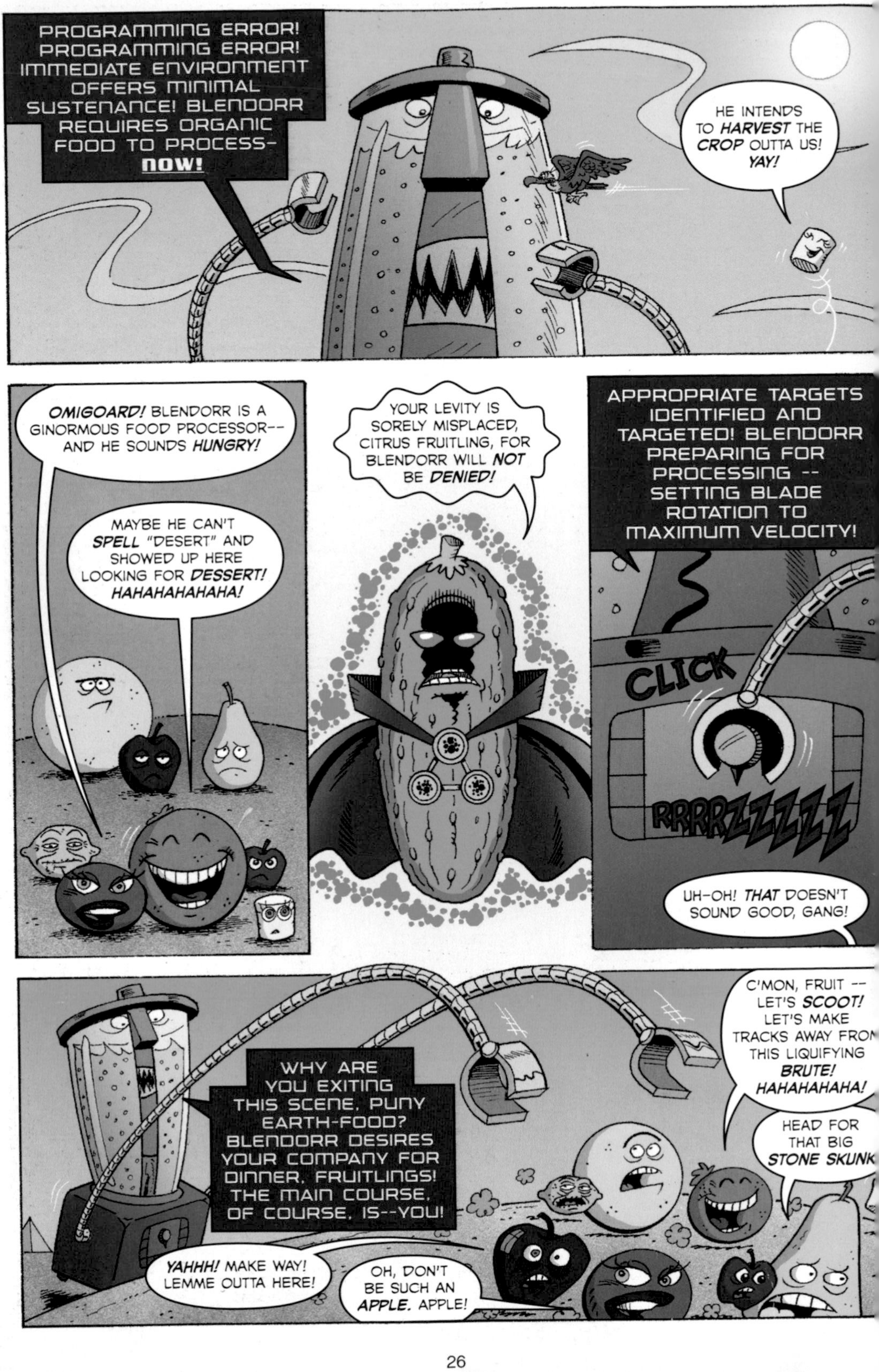
PROGRAMMING ERROR! PROGRAMMING ERROR! IMMEDIATE ENVIRONMENT OFFERS MINIMAL SUSTENANCE! BLENDORR REQUIRES ORGANIC FOOD TO PROCESS-- NOW!
HE INTENDS TO HARVEST THE CROP OUTTA US! YAY!
OMIGOARD! BLENDORR IS A GINORMOUS FOOD PROCESSOR-- AND HE SOUNDS HUNGRY!
MAYBE HE CAN'T SPELL "DESERT" AND SHOWED UP HERE LOOKING FOR DESSERT! HAHAHAHAHAHA!
YOUR LEVITY IS SORELY MISPLACED, CITRUS FRUITLING, FOR BLENDORR WILL NOT BE DENIED!
APPROPRIATE TARGETS IDENTIFIED AND TARGETED! BLENDORR PREPARING FOR PROCESSING -- SETTING BLADE ROTATION TO MAXIMUM VELOCITY!
CLICK
RRRRZZZZZZ
UH-OH! THAT DOESN'T SOUND GOOD, GANG!
WHY ARE YOU EXITING THIS SCENE, PUNY EARTH-FOOD? BLENDORR DESIRES YOUR COMPANY FOR DINNER, FRUITLINGS! THE MAIN COURSE, OF COURSE, IS--YOU!
C'MON, FRUIT -- LET'S SCOOT! LET'S MAKE TRACKS AWAY FROM THIS LIQUIFYING BRUTE! HAHAHAHAHA!
HEAD FOR THAT BIG STONE SKUNK
YAHHH! MAKE WAY! LEMME OUTTA HERE!
OH, DON'T BE SUCH AN APPLE, APPLE!

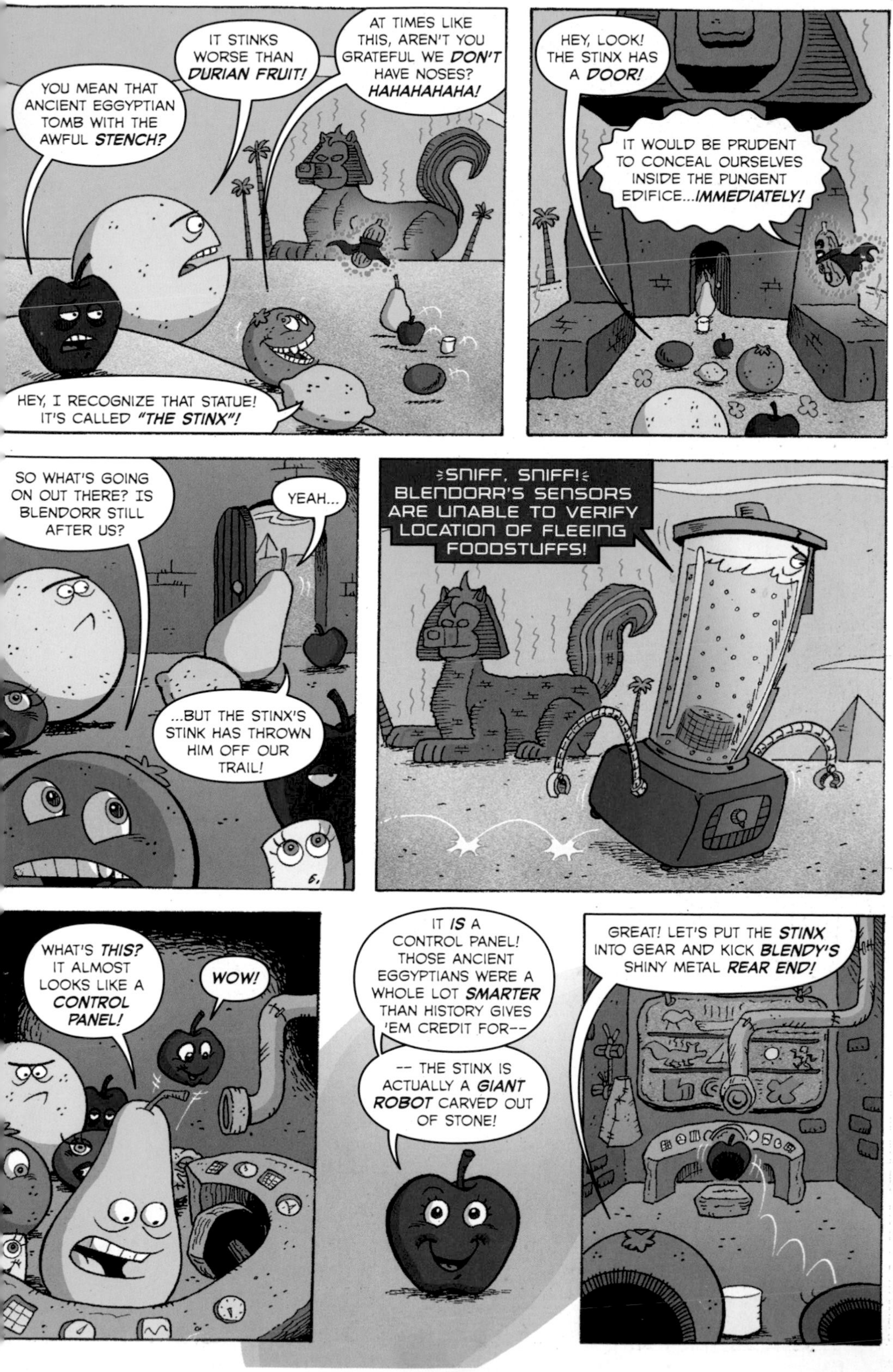
HEY, I RECOGNIZE THAT STATUE! IT'S CALLED "THE STINX"!
YOU MEAN THAT ANCIENT EGGYPTIAN TOMB WITH THE AWFUL STENCH?
IT STINKS WORSE THAN DURIAN FRUIT!
AT TIMES LIKE THIS, AREN'T YOU GRATEFUL WE DON'T HAVE NOSES? HAHAHAHAHA!
HEY, LOOK! THE STINX HAS A DOOR!
IT WOULD BE PRUDENT TO CONCEAL OURSELVES INSIDE THE PUNGENT EDIFICE...IMMEDIATELY!
SO WHAT'S GOING ON OUT THERE? IS BLENDORR STILL AFTER US?
YEAH...
...BUT THE STINX'S STINK HAS THROWN HIM OFF OUR TRAIL!
SNIFF, SNIFF! BLENDORR'S SENSORS ARE UNABLE TO VERIFY LOCATION OF FLEEING FOODSTUFFS!
WHAT'S THIS? IT ALMOST LOOKS LIKE A CONTROL PANEL!
WOW!
IT IS A CONTROL PANEL! THOSE ANCIENT EGGYPTIANS WERE A WHOLE LOT SMARTER THAN HISTORY GIVES 'EM CREDIT FOR--
-- THE STINX IS ACTUALLY A GIANT ROBOT CARVED OUT OF STONE!
GREAT! LET'S PUT THE STINX INTO GEAR AND KICK BLENDY'S SHINY METAL REAR END!

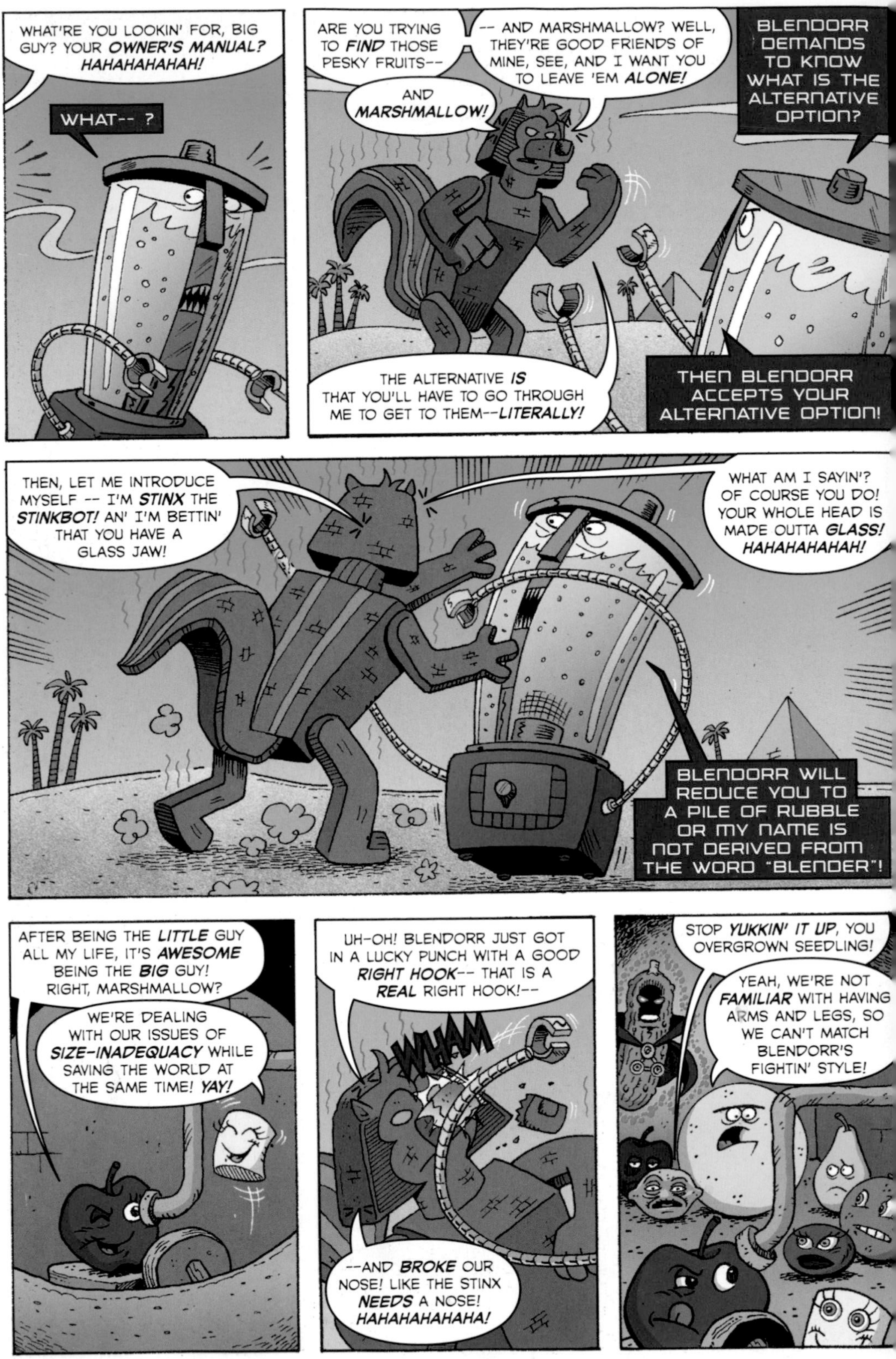
WHAT'RE YOU LOOKIN' FOR, BIG GUY? YOUR OWNER'S MANUAL? HAHAHAHAHAH!
WHAT-- ?
ARE YOU TRYING TO FIND THOSE PESKY FRUITS--
AND MARSHMALLOW!
-- AND MARSHMALLOW? WELL, THEY'RE GOOD FRIENDS OF MINE, SEE, AND I WANT YOU TO LEAVE 'EM ALONE!
BLENDORR DEMANDS TO KNOW WHAT IS THE ALTERNATIVE OPTION?
THE ALTERNATIVE IS THAT YOU'LL HAVE TO GO THROUGH ME TO GET TO THEM--LITERALLY!
THEN BLENDORR ACCEPTS YOUR ALTERNATIVE OPTION!
THEN, LET ME INTRODUCE MYSELF -- I'M STINX THE STINKBOT! AN' I'M BETTIN' THAT YOU HAVE A GLASS JAW!
WHAT AM I SAYIN'? OF COURSE YOU DO! YOUR WHOLE HEAD IS MADE OUTTA GLASS! HAHAHAHAHAH!
BLENDORR WILL REDUCE YOU TO A PILE OF RUBBLE OR MY NAME IS NOT DERIVED FROM THE WORD "BLENDER"!
AFTER BEING THE LITTLE GUY ALL MY LIFE, IT'S AWESOME BEING THE BIG GUY! RIGHT, MARSHMALLOW?
WE'RE DEALING WITH OUR ISSUES OF SIZE-INADEQUACY WHILE SAVING THE WORLD AT THE SAME TIME! YAY!
UH-OH! BLENDORR JUST GOT IN A LUCKY PUNCH WITH A GOOD RIGHT HOOK-- THAT IS A REAL RIGHT HOOK!--
WHAM
--AND BROKE OUR NOSE! LIKE THE STINX NEEDS A NOSE! HAHAHAHAHAHA!
STOP YUKKIN' IT UP, YOU OVERGROWN SEEDLING!
YEAH, WE'RE NOT FAMILIAR WITH HAVING ARMS AND LEGS, SO WE CAN'T MATCH BLENDORR'S FIGHTIN' STYLE!

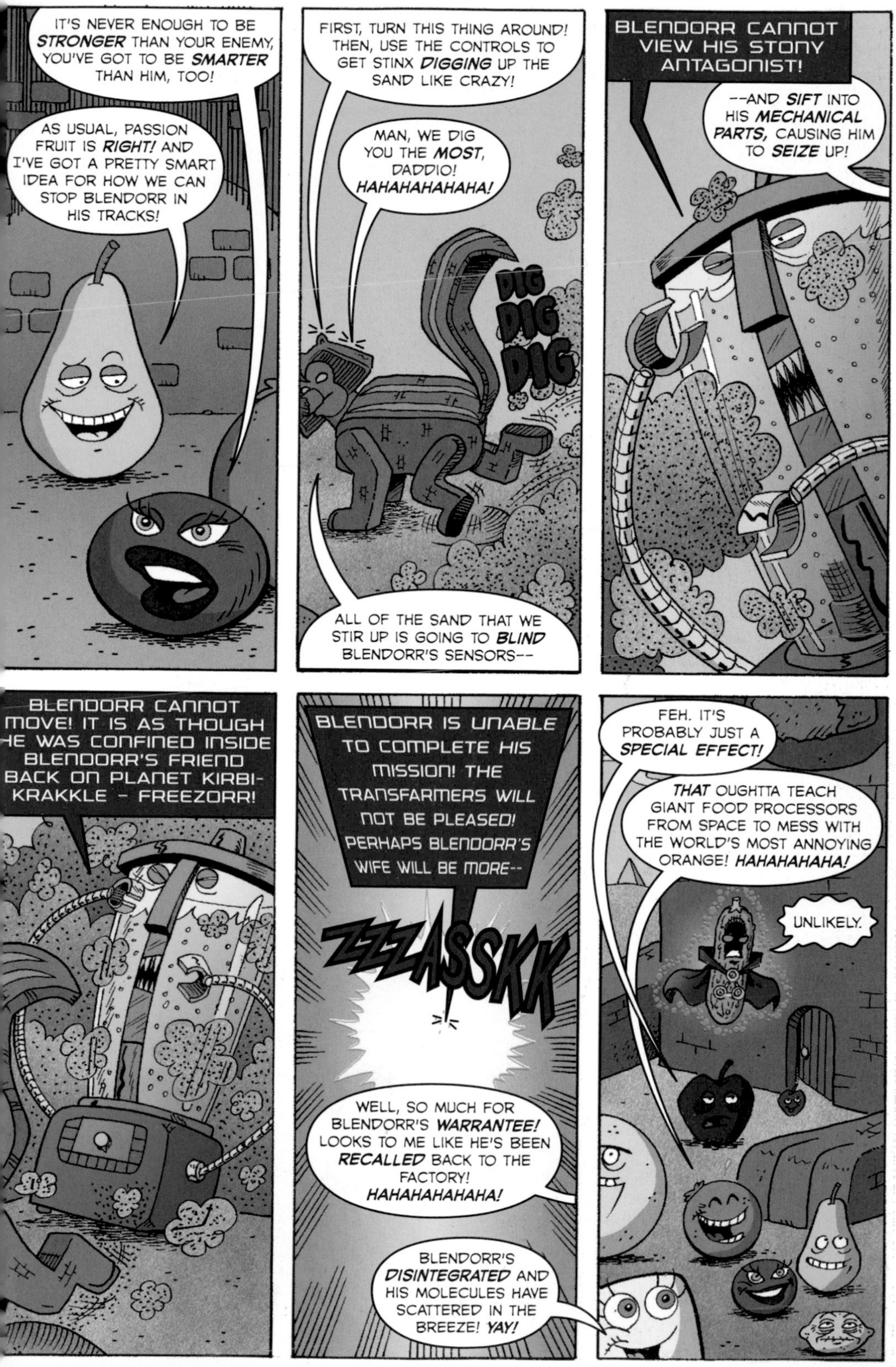
IT'S NEVER ENOUGH TO BE STRONGER THAN YOUR ENEMY, YOU'VE GOT TO BE SMARTER THAN HIM, TOO!
AS USUAL, PASSION FRUIT IS RIGHT! AND I'VE GOT A PRETTY SMART IDEA FOR HOW WE CAN STOP BLENDORR IN HIS TRACKS!
FIRST, TURN THIS THING AROUND! THEN, USE THE CONTROLS TO GET STINX DIGGING UP THE SAND LIKE CRAZY!
MAN, WE DIG YOU THE MOST, DADDIO! HAHAHAHAHAHA!
DIG DIG DIG
ALL OF THE SAND THAT WE STIR UP IS GOING TO BLIND BLENDORR'S SENSORS--
BLENDORR CANNOT VIEW HIS STONY ANTAGONIST!
--AND SIFT INTO HIS MECHANICAL PARTS, CAUSING HIM TO SEIZE UP!
BLENDORR CANNOT MOVE! IT IS AS THOUGH HE WAS CONFINED INSIDE BLENDORR'S FRIEND BACK ON PLANET KIRBI-KRAKKLE - FREEZORR!
BLENDORR IS UNABLE TO COMPLETE HIS MISSION! THE TRANSFARMERS WILL NOT BE PLEASED! PERHAPS BLENDORR'S WIFE WILL BE MORE--
ZZZASSKK
WELL, SO MUCH FOR BLENDORR'S WARRANTEE! LOOKS TO ME LIKE HE'S BEEN RECALLED BACK TO THE FACTORY! HAHAHAHAHAHA!
BLENDORR'S DISINTEGRATED AND HIS MOLECULES HAVE SCATTERED IN THE BREEZE! YAY!
FEH. IT'S PROBABLY JUST A SPECIAL EFFECT!
THAT OUGHTTA TEACH GIANT FOOD PROCESSORS FROM SPACE TO MESS WITH THE WORLD'S MOST ANNOYING ORANGE! HAHAHAHAHA!
UNLIKELY.

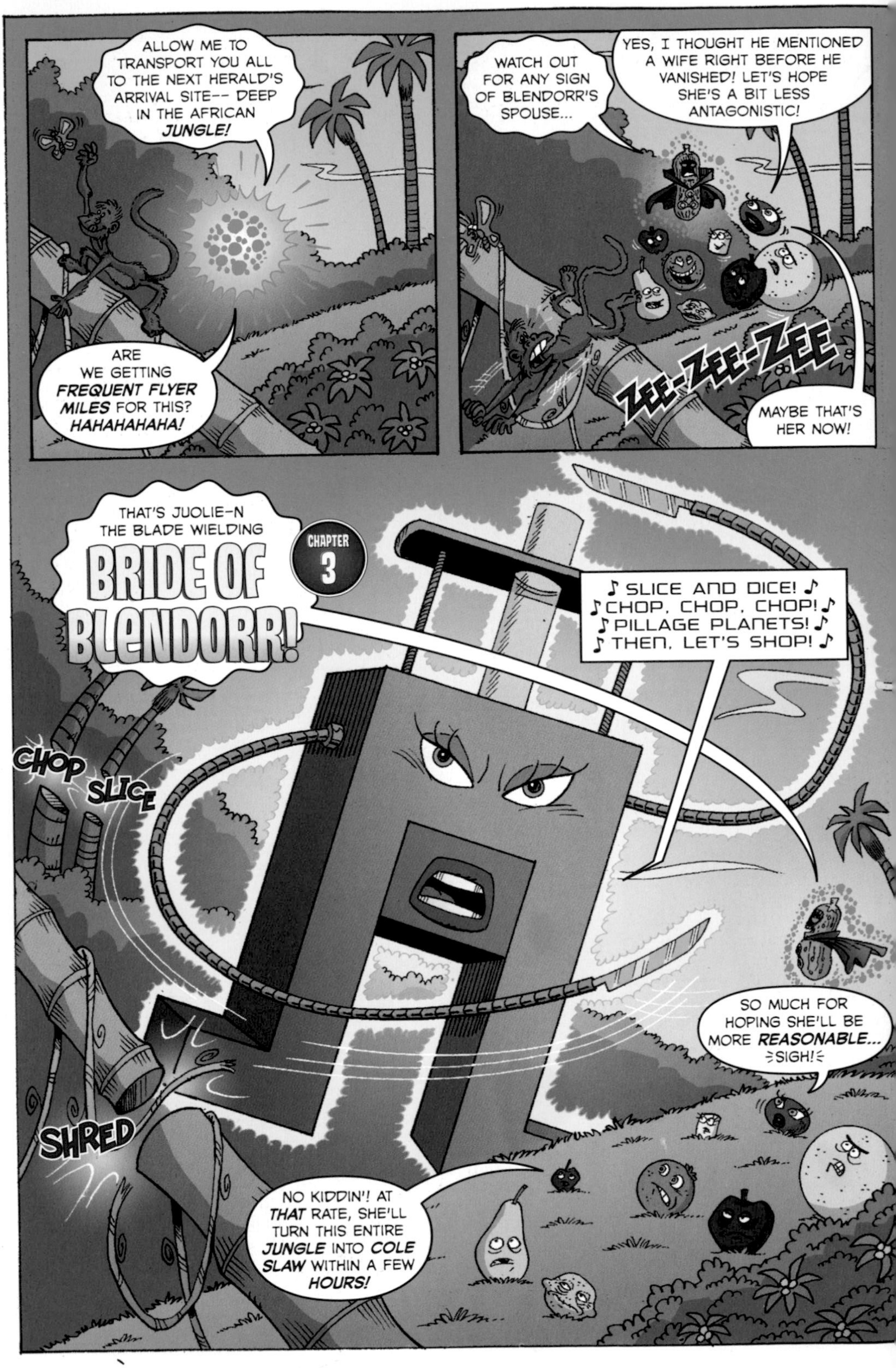
ALLOW ME TO TRANSPORT YOU ALL TO THE NEXT HERALD'S ARRIVAL SITE-- DEEP IN THE AFRICAN JUNGLE!
ARE WE GETTING FREQUENT FLYER MILES FOR THIS? HAHAHAHAHA!
WATCH OUT FOR ANY SIGN OF BLENDORR'S SPOUSE...
YES, I THOUGHT HE MENTIONED A WIFE RIGHT BEFORE HE VANISHED! LET'S HOPE SHE'S A BIT LESS ANTAGONISTIC!
ZEE-ZEE-ZEE
MAYBE THAT'S HER NOW!
THAT'S JUOLIE-N THE BLADE WIELDING
BRIDE OF BLENDORR!
CHAPTER 3
♪ SLICE AND DICE! ♪ ♪ CHOP, CHOP, CHOP! ♪ ♪ PILLAGE PLANETS! ♪ ♪ THEN, LET'S SHOP! ♪
CHOP
SLICE
SHRED
SO MUCH FOR HOPING SHE'LL BE MORE REASONABLE... ≑SIGH!≑
NO KIDDIN'! AT THAT RATE, SHE'LL TURN THIS ENTIRE JUNGLE INTO COLE SLAW WITHIN A FEW HOURS!

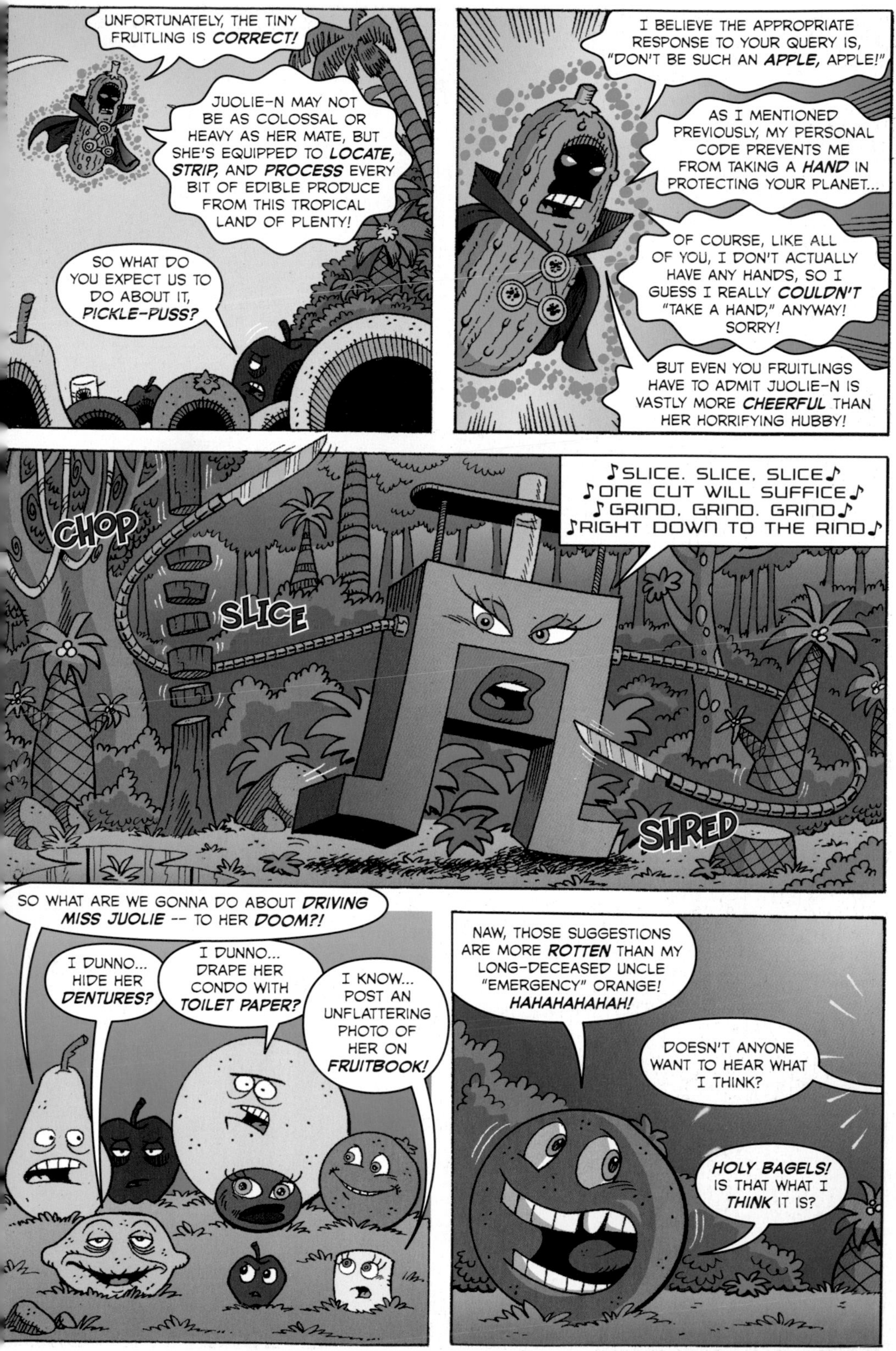

UNFORTUNATELY, THE TINY FRUITLING IS CORRECT!
JUOLIE-N MAY NOT BE AS COLOSSAL OR HEAVY AS HER MATE, BUT SHE'S EQUIPPED TO LOCATE, STRIP, AND PROCESS EVERY BIT OF EDIBLE PRODUCE FROM THIS TROPICAL LAND OF PLENTY!
SO WHAT DO YOU EXPECT US TO DO ABOUT IT, PICKLE-PUSS?
I BELIEVE THE APPROPRIATE RESPONSE TO YOUR QUERY IS, "DON'T BE SUCH AN APPLE, APPLE!"
AS I MENTIONED PREVIOUSLY, MY PERSONAL CODE PREVENTS ME FROM TAKING A HAND IN PROTECTING YOUR PLANET...
OF COURSE, LIKE ALL OF YOU, I DON'T ACTUALLY HAVE ANY HANDS, SO I GUESS I REALLY COULDN'T "TAKE A HAND," ANYWAY! SORRY!
BUT EVEN YOU FRUITLINGS HAVE TO ADMIT JUOLIE-N IS VASTLY MORE CHEERFUL THAN HER HORRIFYING HUBBY!
♪SLICE. SLICE. SLICE♪
♪ONE CUT WILL SUFFICE♪
♪GRIND. GRIND. GRIND♪
♪RIGHT DOWN TO THE RIND♪
CHOP
SLICE
SHRED
SO WHAT ARE WE GONNA DO ABOUT DRIVING MISS JUOLIE -- TO HER DOOM?!
I DUNNO... HIDE HER DENTURES?
I DUNNO... DRAPE HER CONDO WITH TOILET PAPER?
I KNOW... POST AN UNFLATTERING PHOTO OF HER ON FRUITBOOK!
NAW, THOSE SUGGESTIONS ARE MORE ROTTEN THAN MY LONG-DECEASED UNCLE "EMERGENCY" ORANGE! HAHAHAHAHAH!
DOESN'T ANYONE WANT TO HEAR WHAT I THINK?
HOLY BAGELS! IS THAT WHAT I THINK IT IS?

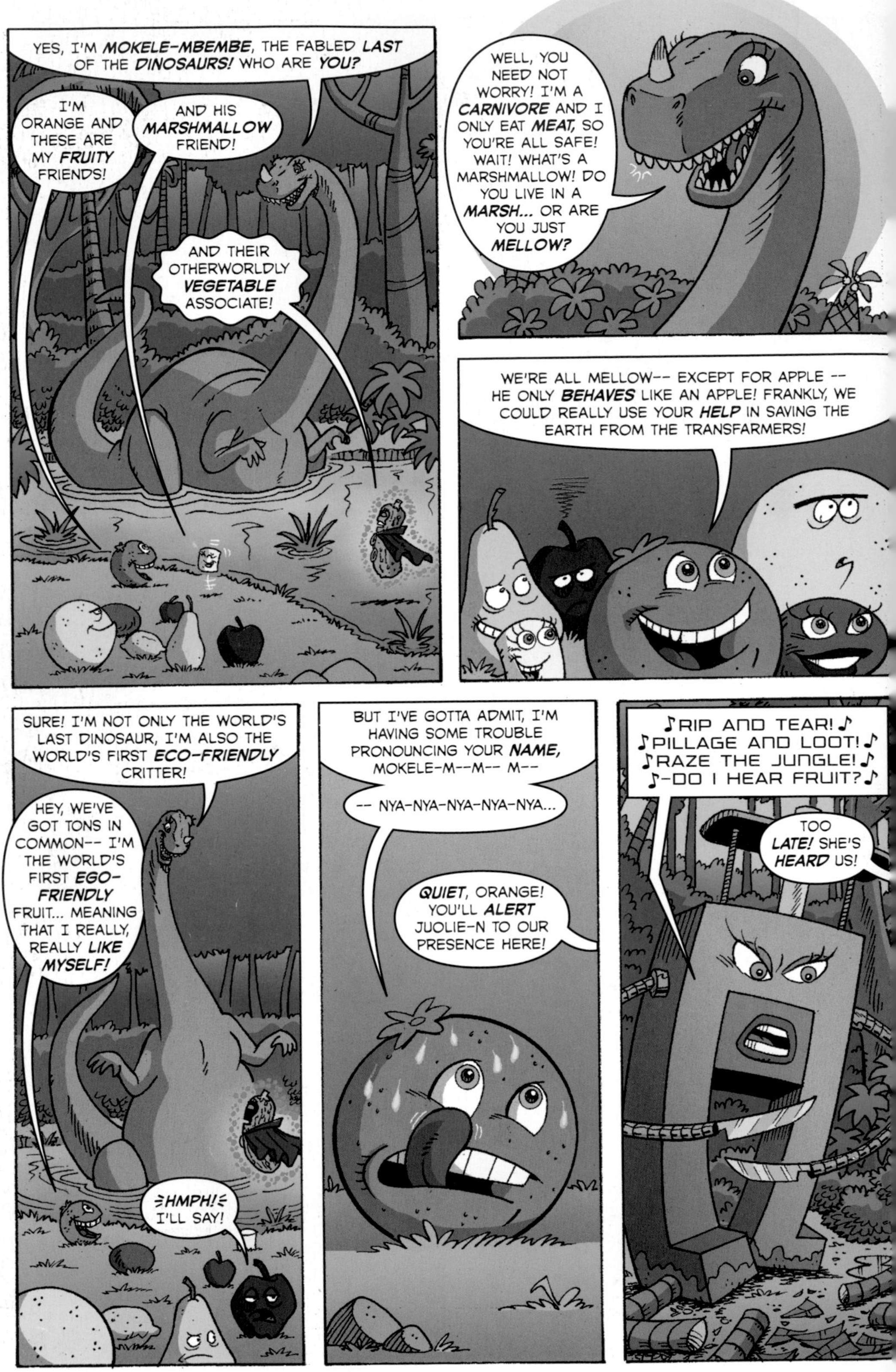

YES, I'M MOKELE-MBEMBE, THE FABLED LAST OF THE DINOSAURS! WHO ARE YOU?
I'M ORANGE AND THESE ARE MY FRUITY FRIENDS!
AND HIS MARSHMALLOW FRIEND!
AND THEIR OTHERWORLDLY VEGETABLE ASSOCIATE!
WELL, YOU NEED NOT WORRY! I'M A CARNIVORE AND I ONLY EAT MEAT, SO YOU'RE ALL SAFE! WAIT! WHAT'S A MARSHMALLOW! DO YOU LIVE IN A MARSH... OR ARE YOU JUST MELLOW?
WE'RE ALL MELLOW-- EXCEPT FOR APPLE -- HE ONLY BEHAVES LIKE AN APPLE! FRANKLY, WE COULD REALLY USE YOUR HELP IN SAVING THE EARTH FROM THE TRANSFARMERS!
SURE! I'M NOT ONLY THE WORLD'S LAST DINOSAUR, I'M ALSO THE WORLD'S FIRST ECO-FRIENDLY CRITTER!
HEY, WE'VE GOT TONS IN COMMON-- I'M THE WORLD'S FIRST EGO-FRIENDLY FRUIT... MEANING THAT I REALLY, REALLY LIKE MYSELF!
HMPH! I'LL SAY!
BUT I'VE GOTTA ADMIT, I'M HAVING SOME TROUBLE PRONOUNCING YOUR NAME, MOKELE-M--M-- M--
-- NYA-NYA-NYA-NYA-NYA...
QUIET, ORANGE! YOU'LL ALERT JUOLIE-N TO OUR PRESENCE HERE!
♪RIP AND TEAR!♪ ♪PILLAGE AND LOOT!♪ ♪RAZE THE JUNGLE!♪ ♪-DO I HEAR FRUIT?♪
TOO LATE! SHE'S HEARD US!

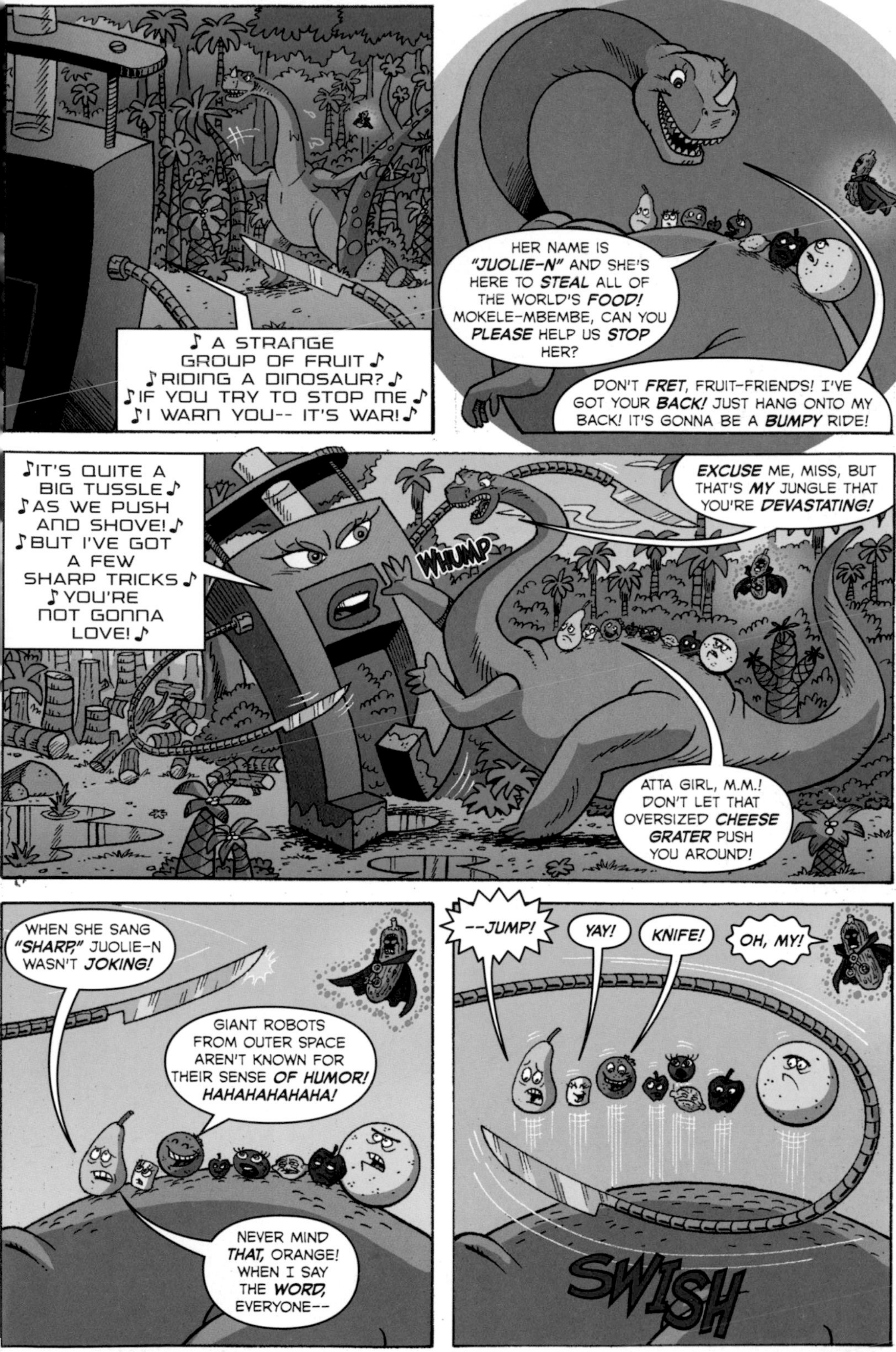
♪ A STRANGE GROUP OF FRUIT ♪
♪ RIDING A DINOSAUR? ♪
♪ IF YOU TRY TO STOP ME ♪
♪ I WARN YOU-- IT'S WAR! ♪
HER NAME IS "JUOLIE-N" AND SHE'S HERE TO STEAL ALL OF THE WORLD'S FOOD! MOKELE-MBEMBE, CAN YOU PLEASE HELP US STOP HER?
DON'T FRET, FRUIT-FRIENDS! I'VE GOT YOUR BACK! JUST HANG ONTO MY BACK! IT'S GONNA BE A BUMPY RIDE!
♪ IT'S QUITE A BIG TUSSLE ♪
♪ AS WE PUSH AND SHOVE! ♪
♪ BUT I'VE GOT A FEW SHARP TRICKS ♪
♪ YOU'RE NOT GONNA LOVE! ♪
WHUMP
EXCUSE ME, MISS, BUT THAT'S MY JUNGLE THAT YOU'RE DEVASTATING!
ATTA GIRL, M.M.! DON'T LET THAT OVERSIZED CHEESE GRATER PUSH YOU AROUND!
WHEN SHE SANG "SHARP," JUOLIE-N WASN'T JOKING!
GIANT ROBOTS FROM OUTER SPACE AREN'T KNOWN FOR THEIR SENSE OF HUMOR! HAHAHAHAHAHA!
NEVER MIND THAT, ORANGE! WHEN I SAY THE WORD, EVERYONE--
--JUMP!
YAY!
KNIFE!
OH, MY!
SWISH

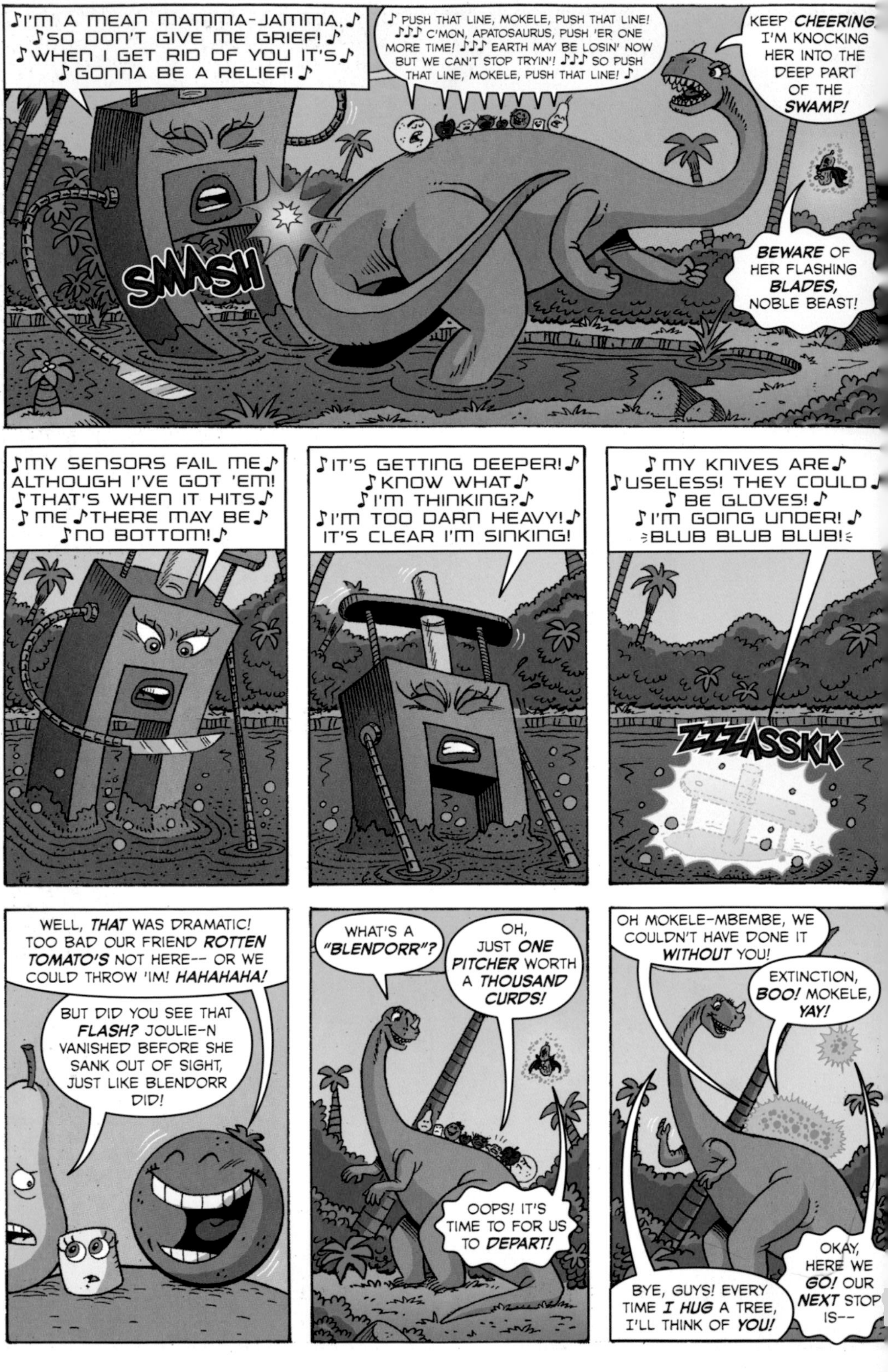
♪I'M A MEAN MAMMA-JAMMA,♪ ♪SO DON'T GIVE ME GRIEF!♪ ♪WHEN I GET RID OF YOU IT'S♪ ♪GONNA BE A RELIEF!♪
♪ PUSH THAT LINE, MOKELE, PUSH THAT LINE! ♪♪♪ C'MON, APATOSAURUS, PUSH 'ER ONE MORE TIME! ♪♪♪ EARTH MAY BE LOSIN' NOW BUT WE CAN'T STOP TRYIN'! ♪♪♪ SO PUSH THAT LINE, MOKELE, PUSH THAT LINE! ♪
KEEP CHEERING, I'M KNOCKING HER INTO THE DEEP PART OF THE SWAMP!
SMASH
BEWARE OF HER FLASHING BLADES, NOBLE BEAST!
♪MY SENSORS FAIL ME♪ ALTHOUGH I'VE GOT 'EM! ♪THAT'S WHEN IT HITS♪ ♪ME♪THERE MAY BE♪ ♪NO BOTTOM!♪
♪IT'S GETTING DEEPER!♪ ♪KNOW WHAT♪ ♪I'M THINKING?♪ ♪I'M TOO DARN HEAVY!♪ IT'S CLEAR I'M SINKING!
♪MY KNIVES ARE♪ ♪USELESS! THEY COULD♪ ♪BE GLOVES!♪ ♪I'M GOING UNDER!♪ BLUB BLUB BLUB!
ZZZASSKK
WELL, THAT WAS DRAMATIC! TOO BAD OUR FRIEND ROTTEN TOMATO'S NOT HERE-- OR WE COULD THROW 'IM! HAHAHAHA!
BUT DID YOU SEE THAT FLASH? JOULIE-N VANISHED BEFORE SHE SANK OUT OF SIGHT, JUST LIKE BLENDORR DID!
WHAT'S A "BLENDORR"?
OH, JUST ONE PITCHER WORTH A THOUSAND CURDS!
OOPS! IT'S TIME TO FOR US TO DEPART!
OH MOKELE-MBEMBE, WE COULDN'T HAVE DONE IT WITHOUT YOU!
EXTINCTION, BOO! MOKELE, YAY!
BYE, GUYS! EVERY TIME I HUG A TREE, I'LL THINK OF YOU!
OKAY, HERE WE GO! OUR NEXT STOP IS--

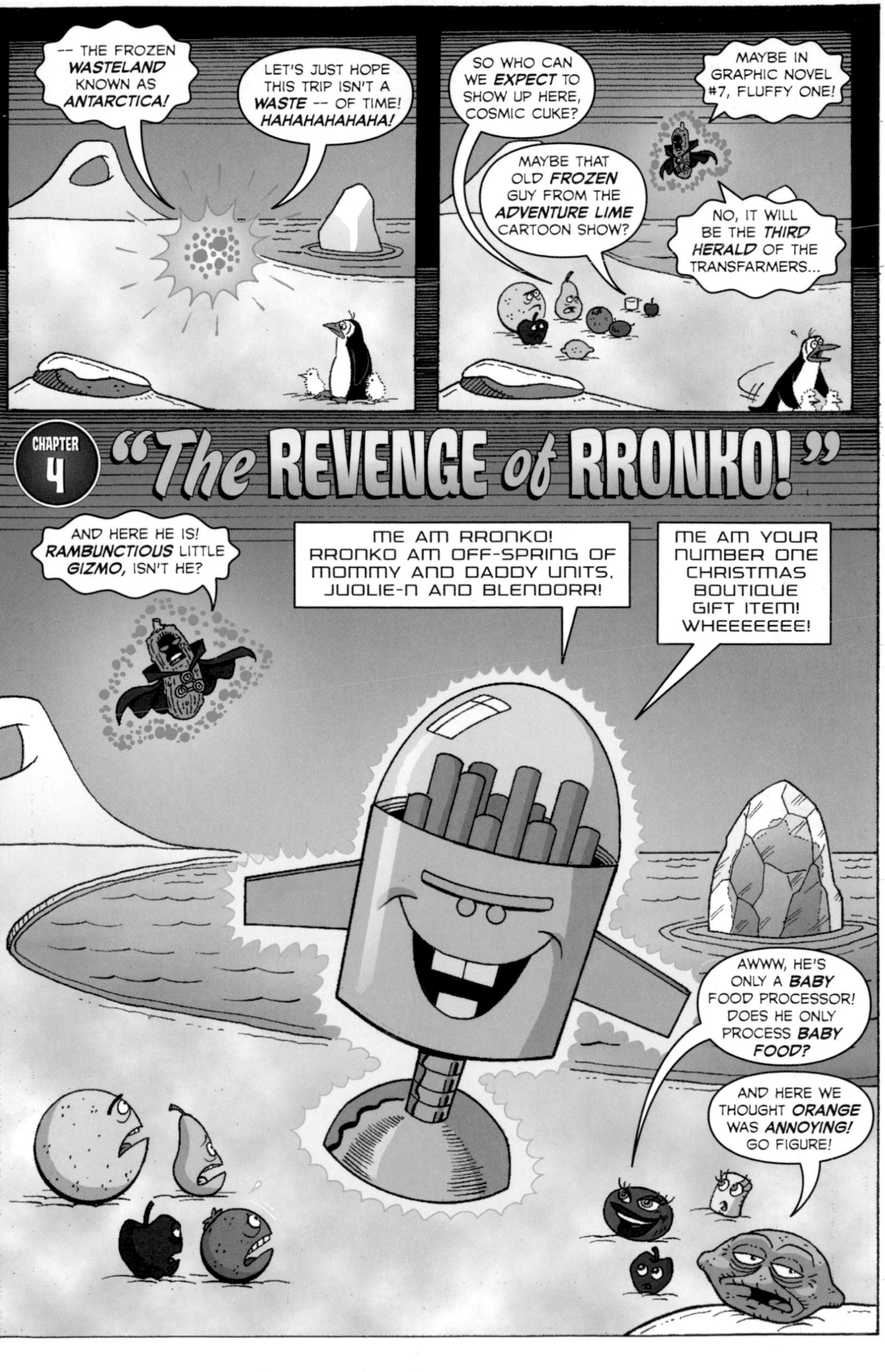
-- THE FROZEN WASTELAND KNOWN AS ANTARCTICA!
LET'S JUST HOPE THIS TRIP ISN'T A WASTE -- OF TIME! HAHAHAHAHAHA!
SO WHO CAN WE EXPECT TO SHOW UP HERE, COSMIC CUKE?
MAYBE THAT OLD FROZEN GUY FROM THE ADVENTURE LIME CARTOON SHOW?
MAYBE IN GRAPHIC NOVEL #7, FLUFFY ONE!
NO, IT WILL BE THE THIRD HERALD OF THE TRANSFARMERS...
CHAPTER 4
"The REVENGE of RRONKO!"
AND HERE HE IS! RAMBUNCTIOUS LITTLE GIZMO, ISN'T HE?
ME AM RRONKO! RRONKO AM OFF-SPRING OF MOMMY AND DADDY UNITS, JUOLIE-N AND BLENDORR!
ME AM YOUR NUMBER ONE CHRISTMAS BOUTIQUE GIFT ITEM! WHEEEEEEE!
AWWW, HE'S ONLY A BABY FOOD PROCESSOR! DOES HE ONLY PROCESS BABY FOOD?
AND HERE WE THOUGHT ORANGE WAS ANNOYING! GO FIGURE!

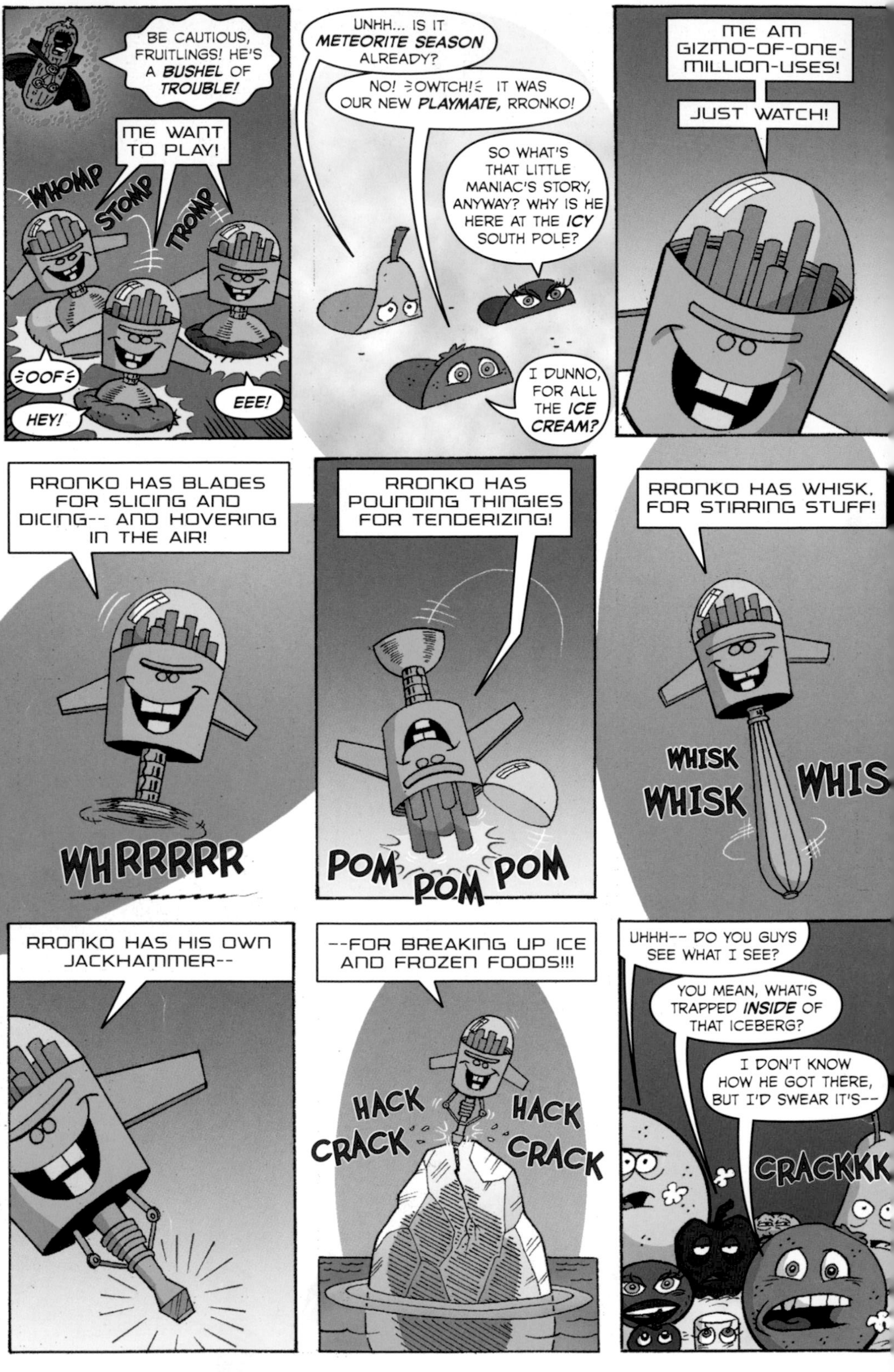
BE CAUTIOUS, FRUITLINGS! HE'S A BUSHEL OF TROUBLE!
ME WANT TO PLAY!
WHOMP
STOMP
TROMP
OOF
HEY!
EEE!
UNHH... IS IT METEORITE SEASON ALREADY?
NO! OWTCH! IT WAS OUR NEW PLAYMATE, RRONKO!
SO WHAT'S THAT LITTLE MANIAC'S STORY, ANYWAY? WHY IS HE HERE AT THE ICY SOUTH POLE?
I DUNNO, FOR ALL THE ICE CREAM?
ME AM GIZMO-OF-ONE-MILLION-USES!
JUST WATCH!
RRONKO HAS BLADES FOR SLICING AND DICING-- AND HOVERING IN THE AIR!
WHRRRRR
RRONKO HAS POUNDING THINGIES FOR TENDERIZING!
POM POM POM
RRONKO HAS WHISK. FOR STIRRING STUFF!
WHISK WHISK WHIS
RRONKO HAS HIS OWN JACKHAMMER--
--FOR BREAKING UP ICE AND FROZEN FOODS!!!
HACK CRACK HACK CRACK
UHHH-- DO YOU GUYS SEE WHAT I SEE?
YOU MEAN, WHAT'S TRAPPED INSIDE OF THAT ICEBERG?
I DON'T KNOW HOW HE GOT THERE, BUT I'D SWEAR IT'S--
CRACKKK

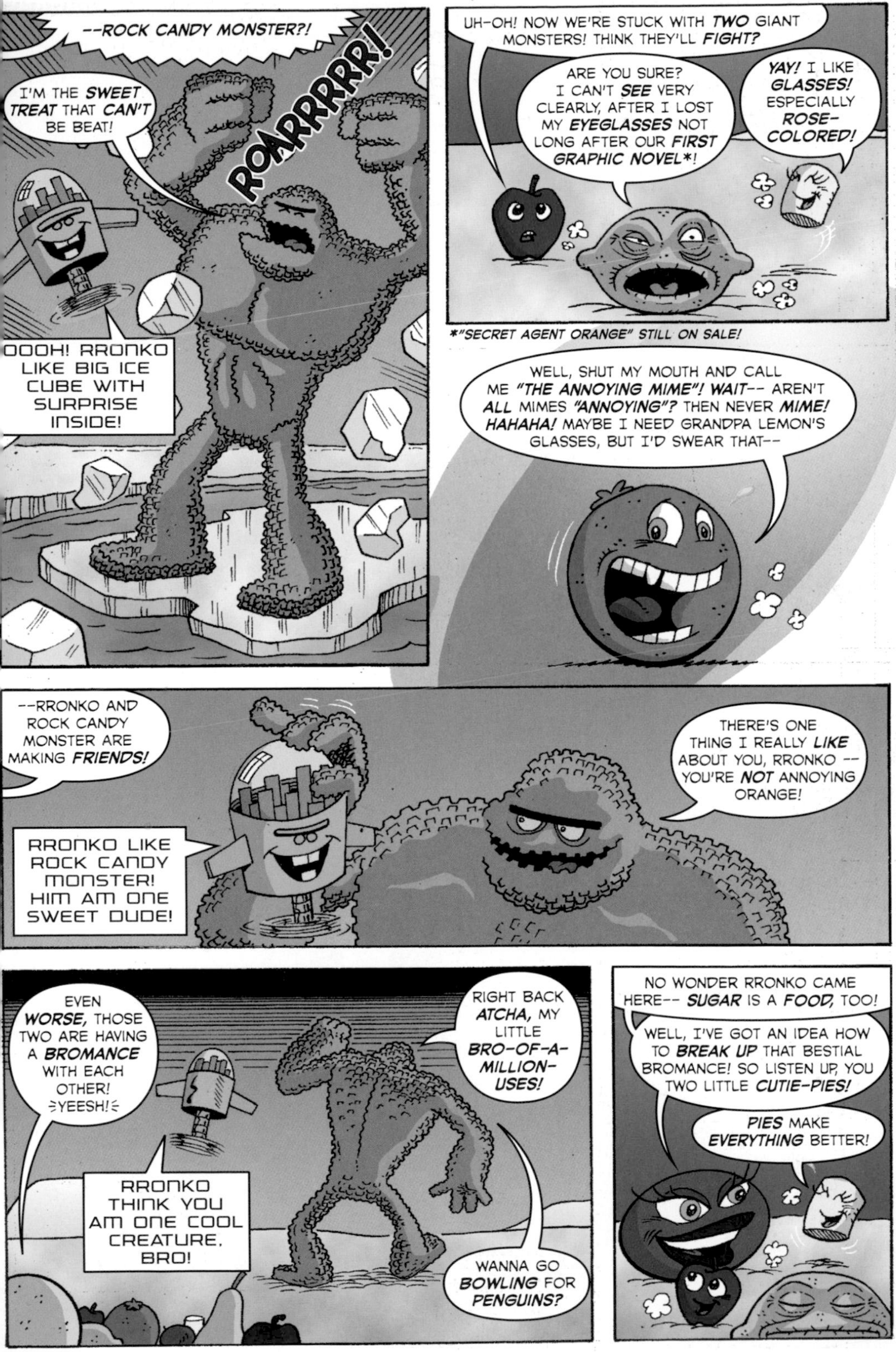
--ROCK CANDY MONSTER?!
ROARRRRR!
I'M THE SWEET TREAT THAT CAN'T BE BEAT!
OOOH! RRONKO LIKE BIG ICE CUBE WITH SURPRISE INSIDE!
UH-OH! NOW WE'RE STUCK WITH TWO GIANT MONSTERS! THINK THEY'LL FIGHT?
ARE YOU SURE? I CAN'T SEE VERY CLEARLY, AFTER I LOST MY EYEGLASSES NOT LONG AFTER OUR FIRST GRAPHIC NOVEL*!
YAY! I LIKE GLASSES! ESPECIALLY ROSE-COLORED!
*"SECRET AGENT ORANGE" STILL ON SALE!
WELL, SHUT MY MOUTH AND CALL ME "THE ANNOYING MIME"! WAIT-- AREN'T ALL MIMES "ANNOYING"? THEN NEVER MIME! HAHAHA! MAYBE I NEED GRANDPA LEMON'S GLASSES, BUT I'D SWEAR THAT--
--RRONKO AND ROCK CANDY MONSTER ARE MAKING FRIENDS!
RRONKO LIKE ROCK CANDY MONSTER! HIM AM ONE SWEET DUDE!
THERE'S ONE THING I REALLY LIKE ABOUT YOU, RRONKO -- YOU'RE NOT ANNOYING ORANGE!
EVEN WORSE, THOSE TWO ARE HAVING A BROMANCE WITH EACH OTHER! YEESH!
RRONKO THINK YOU AM ONE COOL CREATURE, BRO!
RIGHT BACK ATCHA, MY LITTLE BRO-OF-A-MILLION-USES!
WANNA GO BOWLING FOR PENGUINS?
NO WONDER RRONKO CAME HERE-- SUGAR IS A FOOD, TOO!
WELL, I'VE GOT AN IDEA HOW TO BREAK UP THAT BESTIAL BROMANCE! SO LISTEN UP, YOU TWO LITTLE CUTIE-PIES!
PIES MAKE EVERYTHING BETTER!

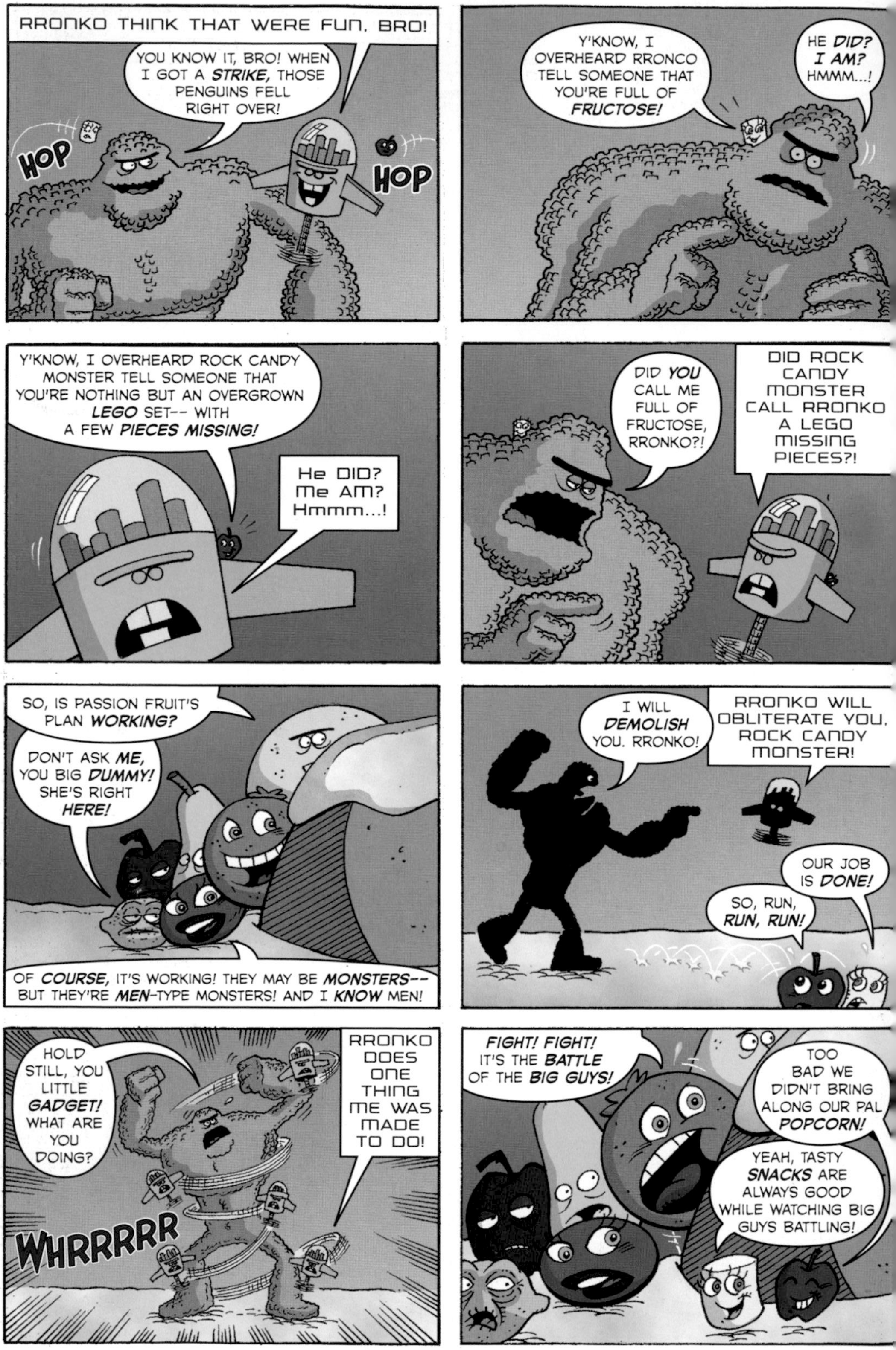
RRONKO THINK THAT WERE FUN, BRO!
YOU KNOW IT, BRO! WHEN I GOT A STRIKE, THOSE PENGUINS FELL RIGHT OVER!
HOP
HOP
Y'KNOW, I OVERHEARD RRONCO TELL SOMEONE THAT YOU'RE FULL OF FRUCTOSE!
HE DID? I AM? HMMM...!
Y'KNOW, I OVERHEARD ROCK CANDY MONSTER TELL SOMEONE THAT YOU'RE NOTHING BUT AN OVERGROWN LEGO SET-- WITH A FEW PIECES MISSING!
He DID? Me AM? Hmmm...!
DID YOU CALL ME FULL OF FRUCTOSE, RRONKO?!
DID ROCK CANDY MONSTER CALL RRONKO A LEGO MISSING PIECES?!
SO, IS PASSION FRUIT'S PLAN WORKING?
DON'T ASK ME, YOU BIG DUMMY! SHE'S RIGHT HERE!
OF COURSE, IT'S WORKING! THEY MAY BE MONSTERS-- BUT THEY'RE MEN-TYPE MONSTERS! AND I KNOW MEN!
I WILL DEMOLISH YOU, RRONKO!
RRONKO WILL OBLITERATE YOU, ROCK CANDY MONSTER!
OUR JOB IS DONE!
SO, RUN, RUN, RUN!
HOLD STILL, YOU LITTLE GADGET! WHAT ARE YOU DOING?
RRONKO DOES ONE THING ME WAS MADE TO DO!
WHRRRRR
FIGHT! FIGHT! IT'S THE BATTLE OF THE BIG GUYS!
TOO BAD WE DIDN'T BRING ALONG OUR PAL POPCORN!
YEAH, TASTY SNACKS ARE ALWAYS GOOD WHILE WATCHING BIG GUYS BATTLING!

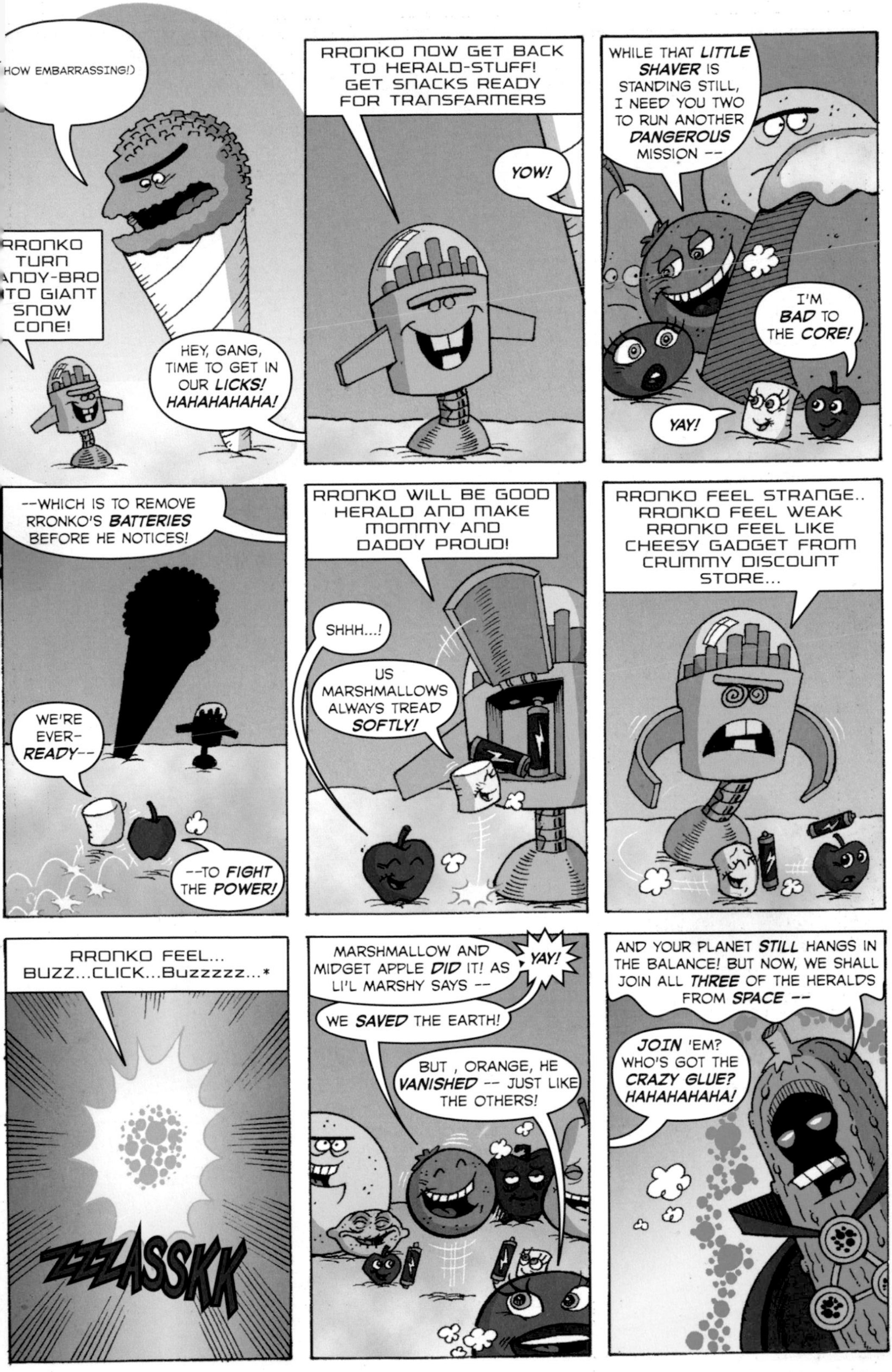

HOW EMBARRASSING!)
RRONKO TURN ANDY-BRO TO GIANT SNOW CONE!
HEY, GANG, TIME TO GET IN OUR LICKS! HAHAHAHAHA!
RRONKO NOW GET BACK TO HERALD-STUFF! GET SNACKS READY FOR TRANSFARMERS
YOW!
WHILE THAT LITTLE SHAVER IS STANDING STILL, I NEED YOU TWO TO RUN ANOTHER DANGEROUS MISSION --
I'M BAD TO THE CORE!
YAY!
--WHICH IS TO REMOVE RRONKO'S BATTERIES BEFORE HE NOTICES!
WE'RE EVER-READY--
--TO FIGHT THE POWER!
RRONKO WILL BE GOOD HERALD AND MAKE MOMMY AND DADDY PROUD!
SHHH...!
US MARSHMALLOWS ALWAYS TREAD SOFTLY!
RRONKO FEEL STRANGE.. RRONKO FEEL WEAK RRONKO FEEL LIKE CHEESY GADGET FROM CRUMMY DISCOUNT STORE...
RRONKO FEEL... BUZZ...CLICK...Buzzzzz...*
ZZZZASSKK
MARSHMALLOW AND MIDGET APPLE DID IT! AS LI'L MARSHY SAYS --
YAY!
WE SAVED THE EARTH!
BUT , ORANGE, HE VANISHED -- JUST LIKE THE OTHERS!
AND YOUR PLANET STILL HANGS IN THE BALANCE! BUT NOW, WE SHALL JOIN ALL THREE OF THE HERALDS FROM SPACE --
JOIN 'EM? WHO'S GOT THE CRAZY GLUE? HAHAHAHAHA!

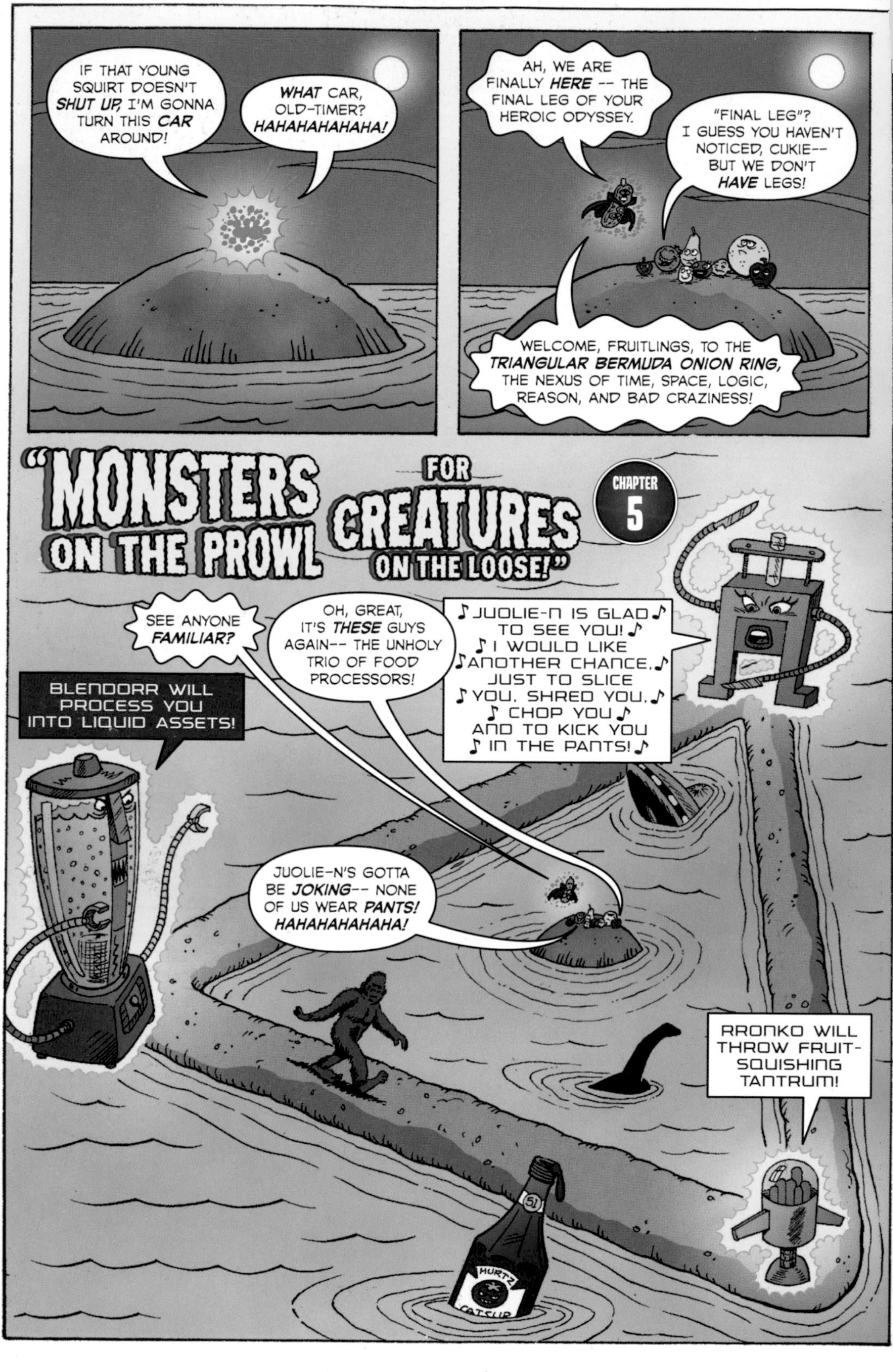
IF THAT YOUNG SQUIRT DOESN'T SHUT UP, I'M GONNA TURN THIS CAR AROUND!
WHAT CAR, OLD-TIMER? HAHAHAHAHAHA!
AH, WE ARE FINALLY HERE -- THE FINAL LEG OF YOUR HEROIC ODYSSEY.
"FINAL LEG"? I GUESS YOU HAVEN'T NOTICED, CUKIE-- BUT WE DON'T HAVE LEGS!
WELCOME, FRUITLINGS, TO THE TRIANGULAR BERMUDA ONION RING, THE NEXUS OF TIME, SPACE, LOGIC, REASON, AND BAD CRAZINESS!
"MONSTERS ON THE PROWL FOR CREATURES ON THE LOOSE!"
CHAPTER 5
SEE ANYONE FAMILIAR?
OH, GREAT, IT'S THESE GUYS AGAIN-- THE UNHOLY TRIO OF FOOD PROCESSORS!
♪ JUOLIE-N IS GLAD ♪ TO SEE YOU! ♪ ♪ I WOULD LIKE ♪ ANOTHER CHANCE. ♪ JUST TO SLICE ♪ YOU, SHRED YOU, ♪ ♪ CHOP YOU ♪ AND TO KICK YOU ♪ IN THE PANTS! ♪
BLENDORR WILL PROCESS YOU INTO LIQUID ASSETS!
JUOLIE-N'S GOTTA BE JOKING-- NONE OF US WEAR PANTS! HAHAHAHAHAHA!
RRONKO WILL THROW FRUIT-SQUISHING TANTRUM!
51
HURTZ
CATSUP

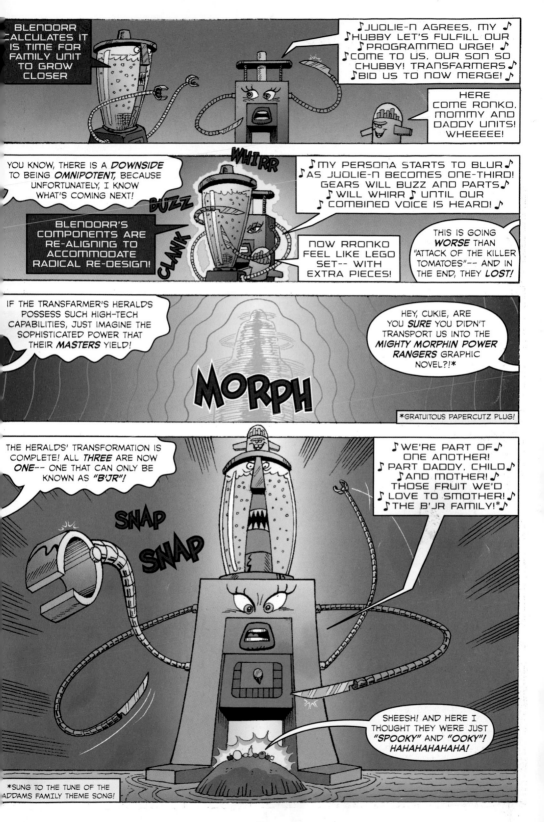

BLENDORR CALCULATES IT IS TIME FOR FAMILY UNIT TO GROW CLOSER

♪JUOLIE-N AGREES, MY ♪ ♪HUBBY LET'S FULFILL OUR ♪ ♪COME TO US, OUR SON SO CHUBBY! TRANSFARMERS ♪ ♪BID US TO NOW MERGE! ♪

HERE COME RONKO, MOMMY AND DADDY UNITS! WHEEEEE!

YOU KNOW, THERE IS A *DOWNSIDE* TO BEING *OMNIPOTENT*, BECAUSE UNFORTUNATELY, I KNOW WHAT'S COMING NEXT!

WHIRR

BUZZ

CLANK

BLENDORR'S COMPONENTS ARE RE-ALIGNING TO ACCOMMODATE RADICAL RE-DESIGN!

♪MY PERSONA STARTS TO BLUR♪ ♪AS JUOLIE-N BECOMES ONE-THIRD! GEARS WILL BUZZ AND PARTS♪ ♪ WILL WHIRR ♪ UNTIL OUR ♪ COMBINED VOICE IS HEARD! ♪

NOW RRONKO FEEL LIKE LEGO SET-- WITH EXTRA PIECES!

THIS IS GOING *WORSE* THAN "ATTACK OF THE KILLER TOMATOES"-- AND IN THE END, THEY *LOST!*

IF THE TRANSFARMER'S HERALDS POSSESS SUCH HIGH-TECH CAPABILITIES, JUST IMAGINE THE SOPHISTICATED POWER THAT THEIR *MASTERS* YIELD!

HEY, CUKIE, ARE YOU *SURE* YOU DIDN'T TRANSPORT US INTO THE *MIGHTY MORPHIN POWER RANGERS* GRAPHIC NOVEL?!*

MORPH

*GRATUITOUS PAPERCUTZ PLUG!

THE HERALDS' TRANSFORMATION IS COMPLETE! ALL *THREE* ARE NOW *ONE*-- ONE THAT CAN ONLY BE KNOWN AS *"B'JR"!*

SNAP

SNAP

♪WE'RE PART OF♪ ONE ANOTHER! ♪ PART DADDY, CHILD ♪ ♪AND MOTHER!♪ THOSE FRUIT WE'D ♪ LOVE TO SMOTHER! ♪THE B'JR FAMILY!*♪

SHEESH! AND HERE I THOUGHT THEY WERE JUST *"SPOOKY"* AND *"OOKY"!* HAHAHAHAHAHA!

*SUNG TO THE TUNE OF THE ADDAMS FAMILY THEME SONG!

41

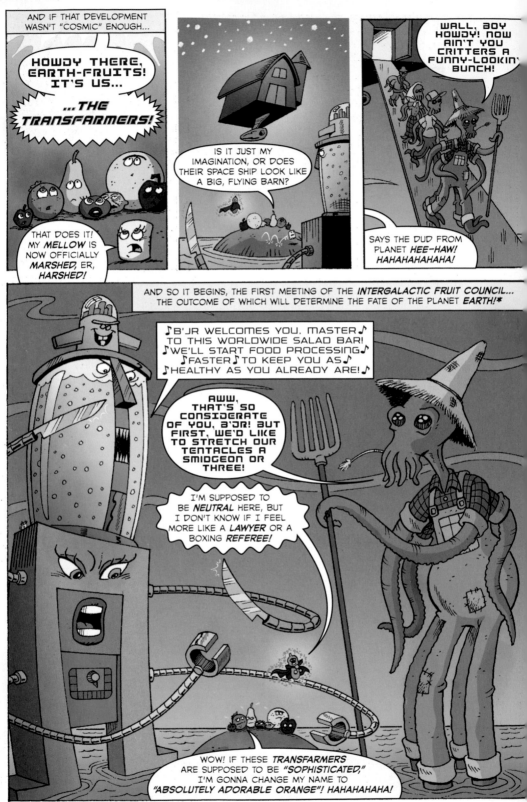

AND IF THAT DEVELOPMENT WASN'T "COSMIC" ENOUGH...

HOWDY THERE, EARTH-FRUITS! IT'S US...

...THE TRANSFARMERS!

THAT DOES IT! MY *MELLOW* IS NOW OFFICIALLY *MARSHED,* ER, *HARSHED!*

IS IT JUST MY IMAGINATION, OR DOES THEIR SPACE SHIP LOOK LIKE A BIG, FLYING BARN?

WALL, BOY HOWDY! NOW AIN'T YOU CRITTERS A FUNNY-LOOKIN' BUNCH!

SAYS THE DUD FROM PLANET *HEE-HAW!* HAHAHAHAHAHA!

AND SO IT BEGINS, THE FIRST MEETING OF THE *INTERGALACTIC FRUIT COUNCIL...* THE OUTCOME OF WHICH WILL DETERMINE THE FATE OF THE PLANET *EARTH!**

♪B'JR WELCOMES YOU, MASTER♪ ♪TO THIS WORLDWIDE SALAD BAR!♪ ♪WE'LL START FOOD PROCESSING♪ ♪FASTER♪ TO KEEP YOU AS♪ ♪HEALTHY AS YOU ALREADY ARE!♪

AWW, THAT'S SO CONSIDERATE OF YOU, B'JR! BUT FIRST, WE'D LIKE TO STRETCH OUR TENTACLES A SMIDGEON OR THREE!

I'M SUPPOSED TO BE *NEUTRAL* HERE, BUT I DON'T KNOW IF I FEEL MORE LIKE A *LAWYER* OR A BOXING *REFEREE!*

WOW! IF THESE *TRANSFARMERS* ARE SUPPOSED TO BE "SOPHISTICATED," I'M GONNA CHANGE MY NAME TO "ABSOLUTELY ADORABLE ORANGE"! HAHAHAHAHA!

*HEY, SMILIN' STAN LEE, HOW'S THAT FOR "COSMIC"?

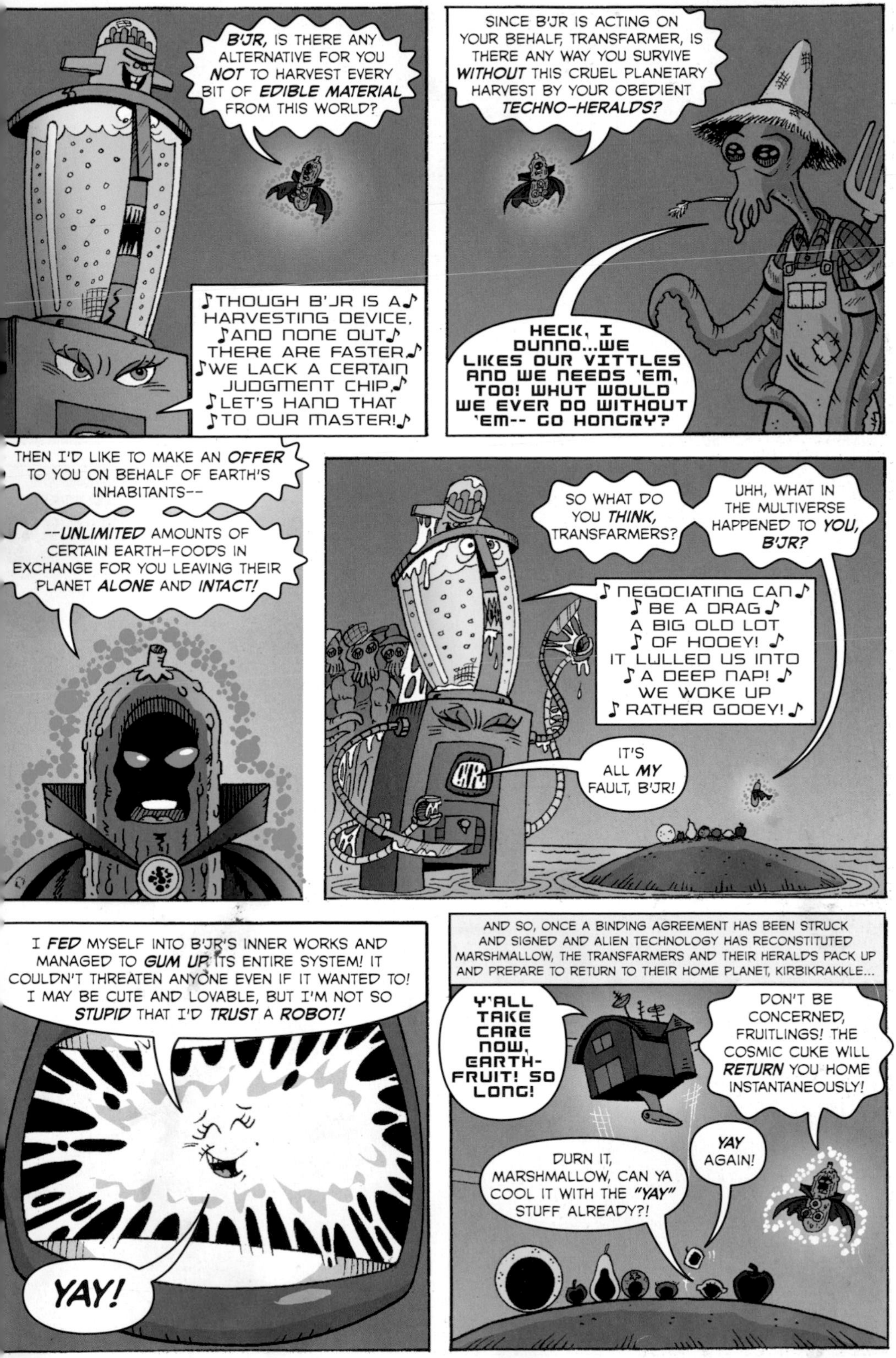

B'JR, IS THERE ANY ALTERNATIVE FOR YOU NOT TO HARVEST EVERY BIT OF EDIBLE MATERIAL FROM THIS WORLD?
♪THOUGH B'JR IS A♪ HARVESTING DEVICE, ♪AND NONE OUT♪ THERE ARE FASTER,♪ ♪WE LACK A CERTAIN JUDGMENT CHIP,♪ ♪LET'S HAND THAT ♪TO OUR MASTER!♪
SINCE B'JR IS ACTING ON YOUR BEHALF, TRANSFARMER, IS THERE ANY WAY YOU SURVIVE WITHOUT THIS CRUEL PLANETARY HARVEST BY YOUR OBEDIENT TECHNO-HERALDS?
HECK, I DUNNO...WE LIKES OUR VITTLES AND WE NEEDS 'EM, TOO! WHUT WOULD WE EVER DO WITHOUT 'EM-- GO HONGRY?
THEN I'D LIKE TO MAKE AN OFFER TO YOU ON BEHALF OF EARTH'S INHABITANTS--
--UNLIMITED AMOUNTS OF CERTAIN EARTH-FOODS IN EXCHANGE FOR YOU LEAVING THEIR PLANET ALONE AND INTACT!
SO WHAT DO YOU THINK, TRANSFARMERS?
UHH, WHAT IN THE MULTIVERSE HAPPENED TO YOU, B'JR?
♪ NEGOCIATING CAN♪ ♪ BE A DRAG♪ A BIG OLD LOT ♪ OF HOOEY! ♪ IT LULLED US INTO ♪ A DEEP NAP! ♪ WE WOKE UP ♪ RATHER GOOEY! ♪
IT'S ALL MY FAULT, B'JR!
I FED MYSELF INTO B'JR'S INNER WORKS AND MANAGED TO GUM UP ITS ENTIRE SYSTEM! IT COULDN'T THREATEN ANYONE EVEN IF IT WANTED TO! I MAY BE CUTE AND LOVABLE, BUT I'M NOT SO STUPID THAT I'D TRUST A ROBOT!
YAY!
AND SO, ONCE A BINDING AGREEMENT HAS BEEN STRUCK AND SIGNED AND ALIEN TECHNOLOGY HAS RECONSTITUTED MARSHMALLOW, THE TRANSFARMERS AND THEIR HERALDS PACK UP AND PREPARE TO RETURN TO THEIR HOME PLANET, KIRBIKRAKKLE...
Y'ALL TAKE CARE NOW, EARTH-FRUIT! SO LONG!
DON'T BE CONCERNED, FRUITLINGS! THE COSMIC CUKE WILL RETURN YOU HOME INSTANTANEOUSLY!
YAY AGAIN!
DURN IT, MARSHMALLOW, CAN YA COOL IT WITH THE "YAY" STUFF ALREADY?!

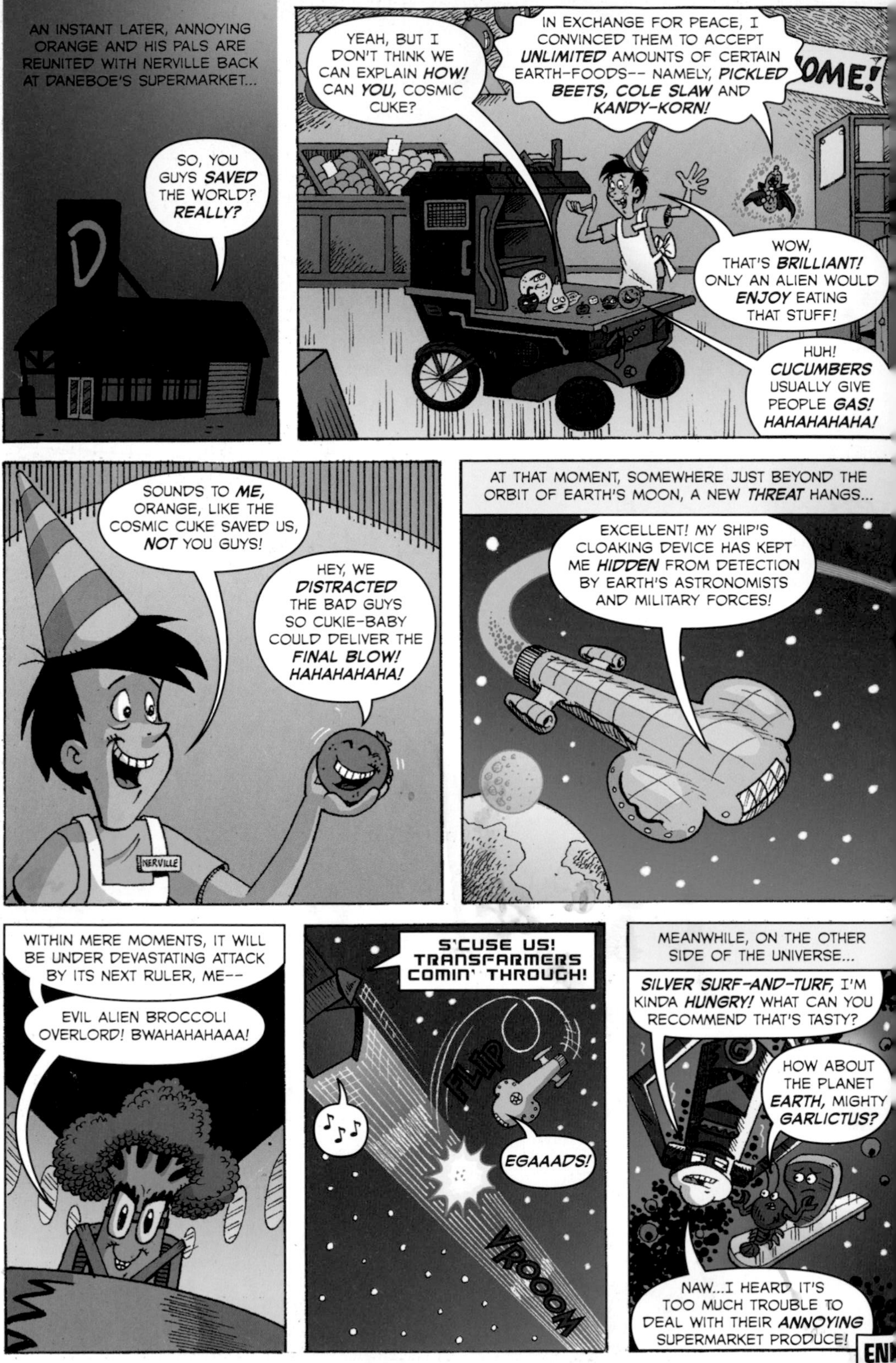
AN INSTANT LATER, ANNOYING ORANGE AND HIS PALS ARE REUNITED WITH NERVILLE BACK AT DANEBOE'S SUPERMARKET...
SO, YOU GUYS SAVED THE WORLD? REALLY?
YEAH, BUT I DON'T THINK WE CAN EXPLAIN HOW! CAN YOU, COSMIC CUKE?
IN EXCHANGE FOR PEACE, I CONVINCED THEM TO ACCEPT UNLIMITED AMOUNTS OF CERTAIN EARTH-FOODS-- NAMELY, PICKLED BEETS, COLE SLAW AND KANDY-KORN!
OME!
WOW, THAT'S BRILLIANT! ONLY AN ALIEN WOULD ENJOY EATING THAT STUFF!
HUH! CUCUMBERS USUALLY GIVE PEOPLE GAS! HAHAHAHAHA!
SOUNDS TO ME, ORANGE, LIKE THE COSMIC CUKE SAVED US, NOT YOU GUYS!
HEY, WE DISTRACTED THE BAD GUYS SO CUKIE-BABY COULD DELIVER THE FINAL BLOW! HAHAHAHAHA!
NERVILLE
AT THAT MOMENT, SOMEWHERE JUST BEYOND THE ORBIT OF EARTH'S MOON, A NEW THREAT HANGS...
EXCELLENT! MY SHIP'S CLOAKING DEVICE HAS KEPT ME HIDDEN FROM DETECTION BY EARTH'S ASTRONOMISTS AND MILITARY FORCES!
WITHIN MERE MOMENTS, IT WILL BE UNDER DEVASTATING ATTACK BY ITS NEXT RULER, ME--
EVIL ALIEN BROCCOLI OVERLORD! BWAHAHAHAAA!
S'CUSE US! TRANSFARMERS COMIN' THROUGH!
♪♪♪
FLIP
EGAAADS!
VROOOOM
MEANWHILE, ON THE OTHER SIDE OF THE UNIVERSE...
SILVER SURF-AND-TURF, I'M KINDA HUNGRY! WHAT CAN YOU RECOMMEND THAT'S TASTY?
HOW ABOUT THE PLANET EARTH, MIGHTY GARLICTUS?
NAW...I HEARD IT'S TOO MUCH TROUBLE TO DEAL WITH THEIR ANNOYING SUPERMARKET PRODUCE!
EN

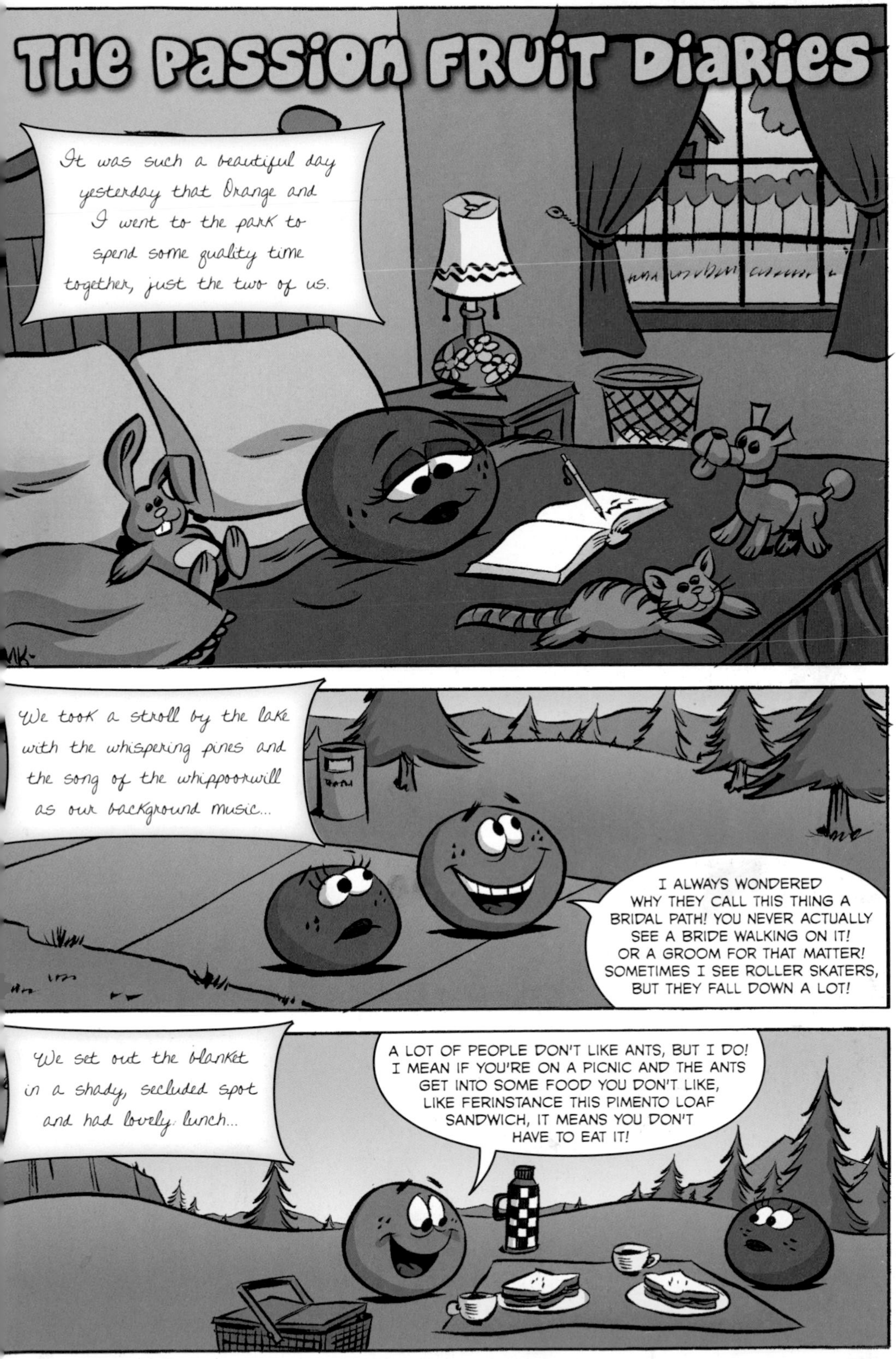
THE PASSION FRUIT DIARIES
It was such a beautiful day yesterday that Orange and I went to the park to spend some quality time together, just the two of us.
We took a stroll by the lake with the whispering pines and the song of the whippoorwill as our background music...
I ALWAYS WONDERED WHY THEY CALL THIS THING A BRIDAL PATH! YOU NEVER ACTUALLY SEE A BRIDE WALKING ON IT! OR A GROOM FOR THAT MATTER! SOMETIMES I SEE ROLLER SKATERS, BUT THEY FALL DOWN A LOT!
We set out the blanket in a shady, secluded spot and had lovely lunch...
A LOT OF PEOPLE DON'T LIKE ANTS, BUT I DO! I MEAN IF YOU'RE ON A PICNIC AND THE ANTS GET INTO SOME FOOD YOU DON'T LIKE, LIKE FERINSTANCE THIS PIMENTO LOAF SANDWICH, IT MEANS YOU DON'T HAVE TO EAT IT!

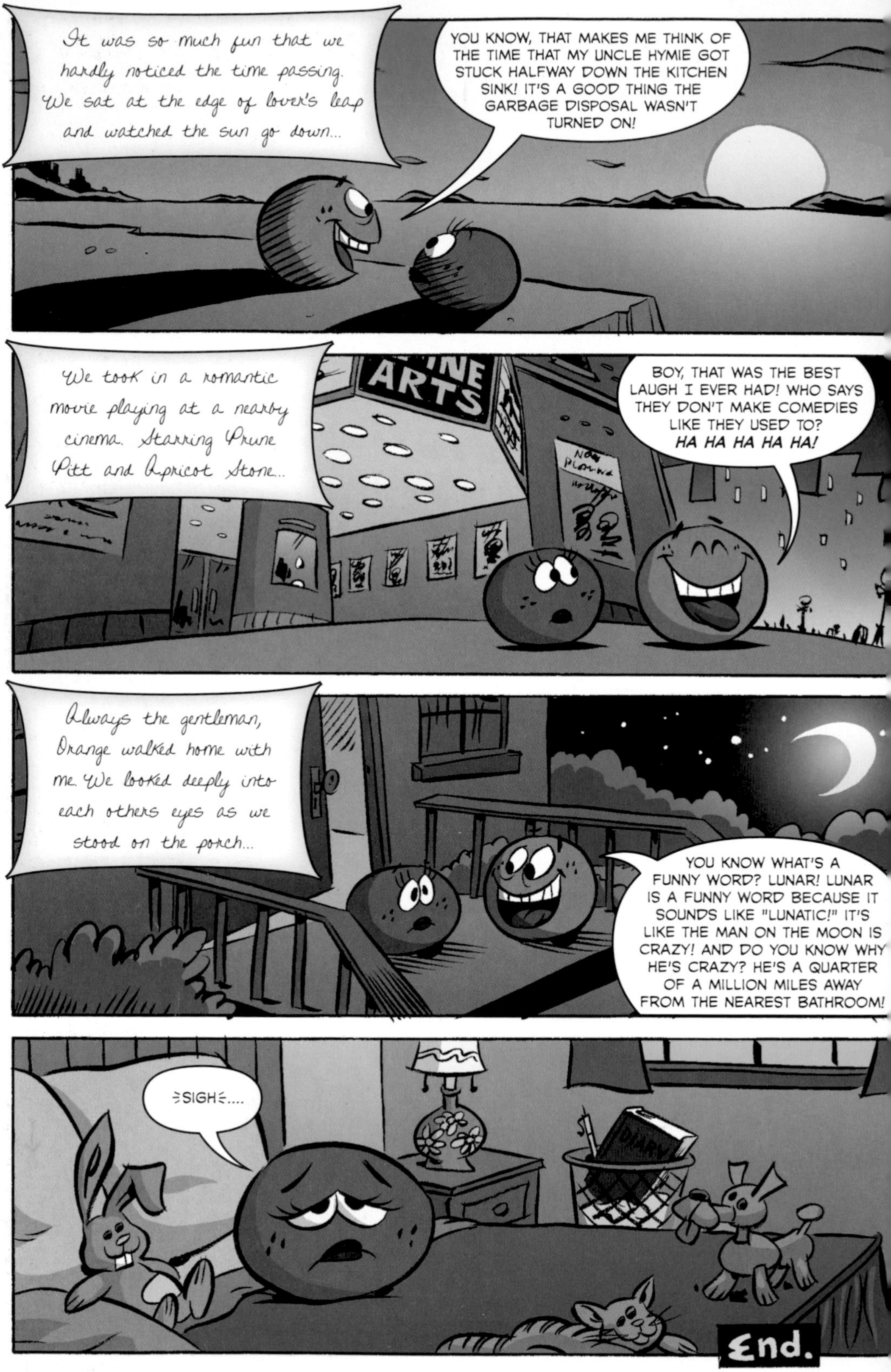
It was so much fun that we hardly noticed the time passing. We sat at the edge of lover's leap and watched the sun go down...
YOU KNOW, THAT MAKES ME THINK OF THE TIME THAT MY UNCLE HYMIE GOT STUCK HALFWAY DOWN THE KITCHEN SINK! IT'S A GOOD THING THE GARBAGE DISPOSAL WASN'T TURNED ON!
We took in a romantic movie playing at a nearby cinema. Starring Prune Pitt and Apricot Stone...
ARTS
BOY, THAT WAS THE BEST LAUGH I EVER HAD! WHO SAYS THEY DON'T MAKE COMEDIES LIKE THEY USED TO? HA HA HA HA HA!
Always the gentleman, Orange walked home with me. We looked deeply into each others eyes as we stood on the porch...
YOU KNOW WHAT'S A FUNNY WORD? LUNAR! LUNAR IS A FUNNY WORD BECAUSE IT SOUNDS LIKE "LUNATIC!" IT'S LIKE THE MAN ON THE MOON IS CRAZY! AND DO YOU KNOW WHY HE'S CRAZY? HE'S A QUARTER OF A MILLION MILES AWAY FROM THE NEAREST BATHROOM!
SIGH....
DIARY
End.

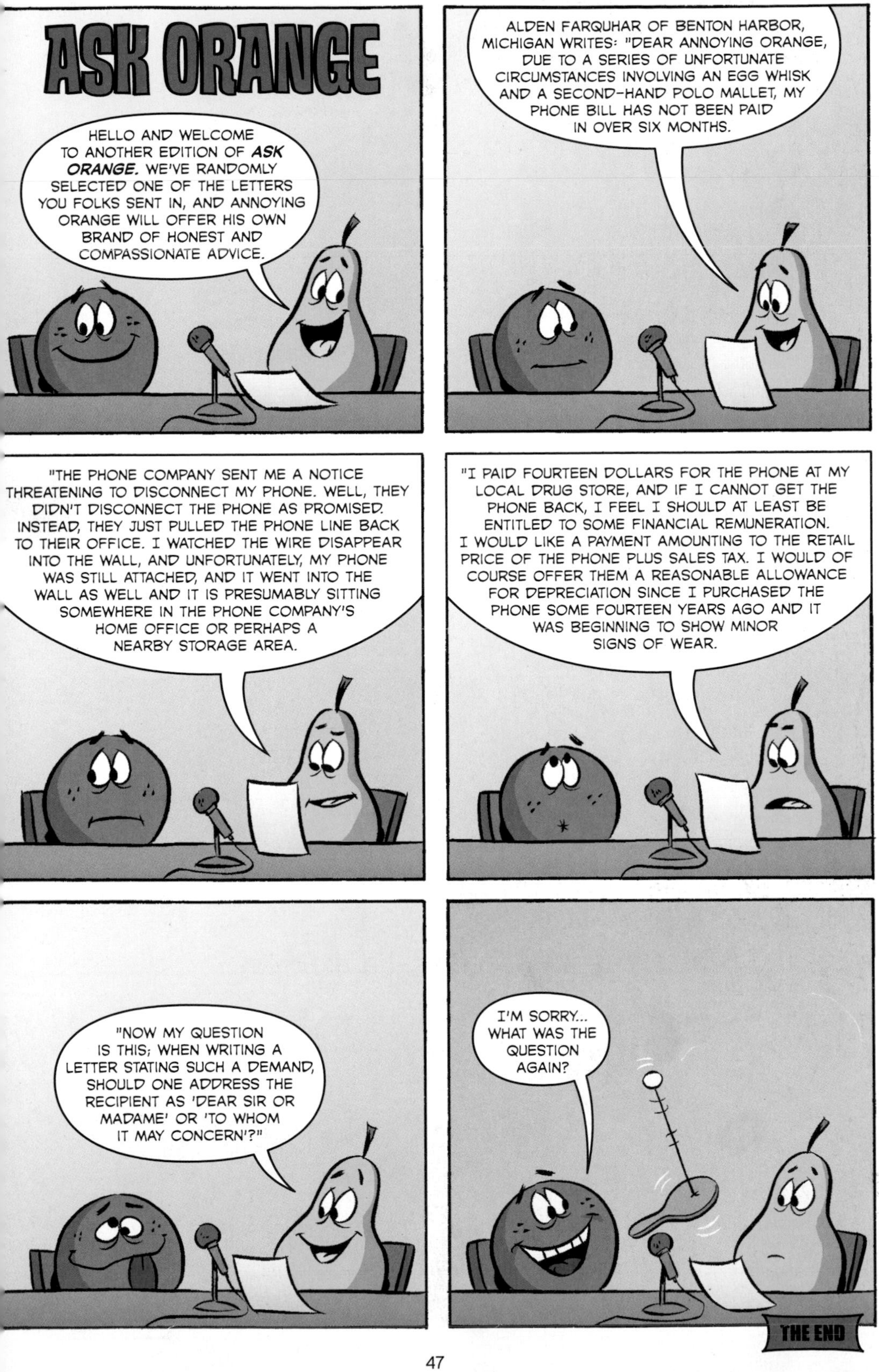
ASK ORANGE
HELLO AND WELCOME TO ANOTHER EDITION OF ASK ORANGE. WE'VE RANDOMLY SELECTED ONE OF THE LETTERS YOU FOLKS SENT IN, AND ANNOYING ORANGE WILL OFFER HIS OWN BRAND OF HONEST AND COMPASSIONATE ADVICE.
ALDEN FARQUHAR OF BENTON HARBOR, MICHIGAN WRITES: "DEAR ANNOYING ORANGE, DUE TO A SERIES OF UNFORTUNATE CIRCUMSTANCES INVOLVING AN EGG WHISK AND A SECOND-HAND POLO MALLET, MY PHONE BILL HAS NOT BEEN PAID IN OVER SIX MONTHS.
"THE PHONE COMPANY SENT ME A NOTICE THREATENING TO DISCONNECT MY PHONE. WELL, THEY DIDN'T DISCONNECT THE PHONE AS PROMISED. INSTEAD, THEY JUST PULLED THE PHONE LINE BACK TO THEIR OFFICE. I WATCHED THE WIRE DISAPPEAR INTO THE WALL, AND UNFORTUNATELY, MY PHONE WAS STILL ATTACHED, AND IT WENT INTO THE WALL AS WELL AND IT IS PRESUMABLY SITTING SOMEWHERE IN THE PHONE COMPANY'S HOME OFFICE OR PERHAPS A NEARBY STORAGE AREA.
"I PAID FOURTEEN DOLLARS FOR THE PHONE AT MY LOCAL DRUG STORE, AND IF I CANNOT GET THE PHONE BACK, I FEEL I SHOULD AT LEAST BE ENTITLED TO SOME FINANCIAL REMUNERATION. I WOULD LIKE A PAYMENT AMOUNTING TO THE RETAIL PRICE OF THE PHONE PLUS SALES TAX. I WOULD OF COURSE OFFER THEM A REASONABLE ALLOWANCE FOR DEPRECIATION SINCE I PURCHASED THE PHONE SOME FOURTEEN YEARS AGO AND IT WAS BEGINNING TO SHOW MINOR SIGNS OF WEAR.
"NOW MY QUESTION IS THIS; WHEN WRITING A LETTER STATING SUCH A DEMAND, SHOULD ONE ADDRESS THE RECIPIENT AS 'DEAR SIR OR MADAME' OR 'TO WHOM IT MAY CONCERN'?"
I'M SORRY... WHAT WAS THE QUESTION AGAIN?
THE END

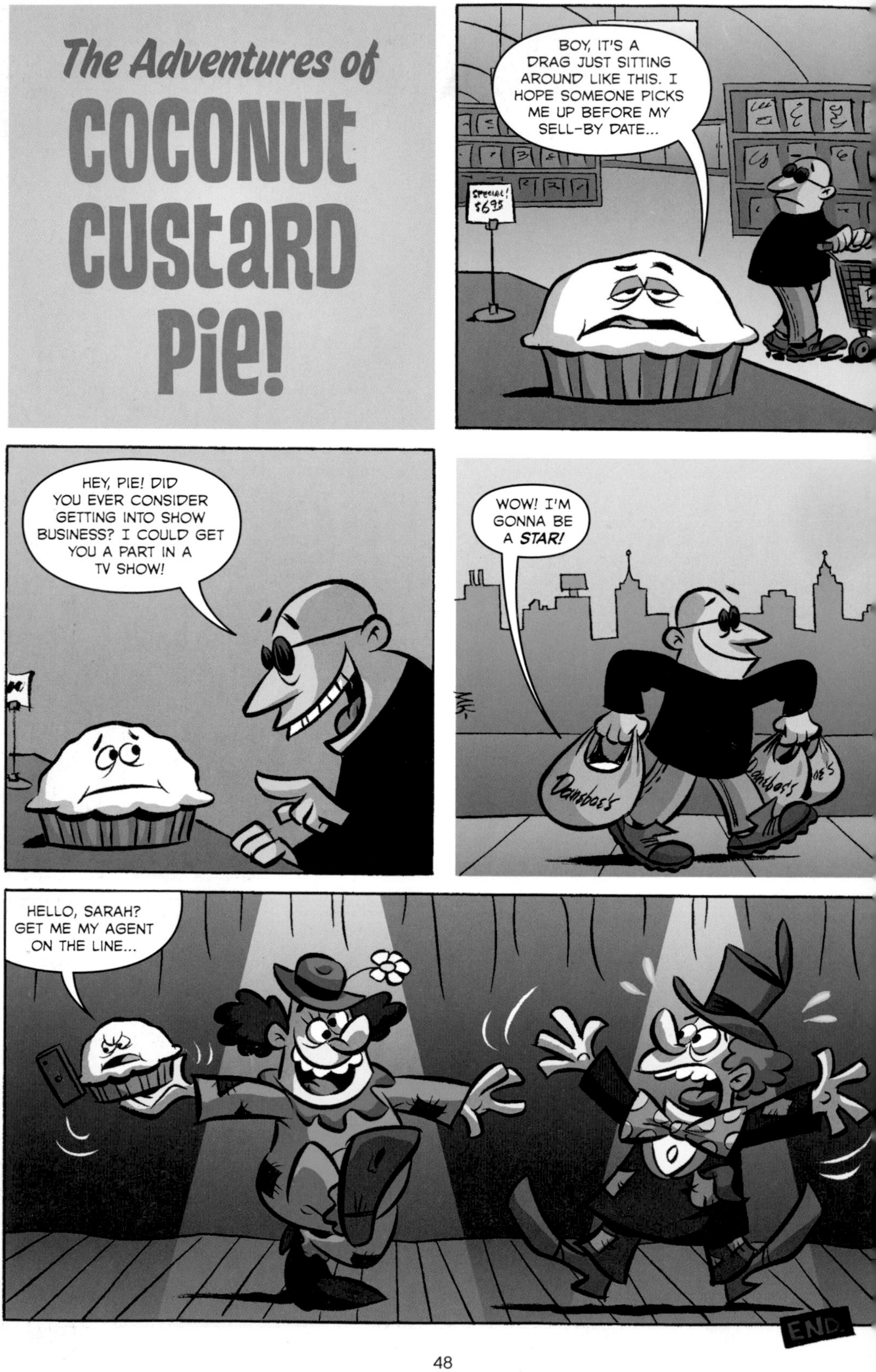
The Adventures of
COCONUT CUSTARD PIE!
BOY, IT'S A DRAG JUST SITTING AROUND LIKE THIS. I HOPE SOMEONE PICKS ME UP BEFORE MY SELL-BY DATE...
SPECIAL! $6.95
HEY, PIE! DID YOU EVER CONSIDER GETTING INTO SHOW BUSINESS? I COULD GET YOU A PART IN A TV SHOW!
WOW! I'M GONNA BE A STAR!
HELLO, SARAH? GET ME MY AGENT ON THE LINE...
END

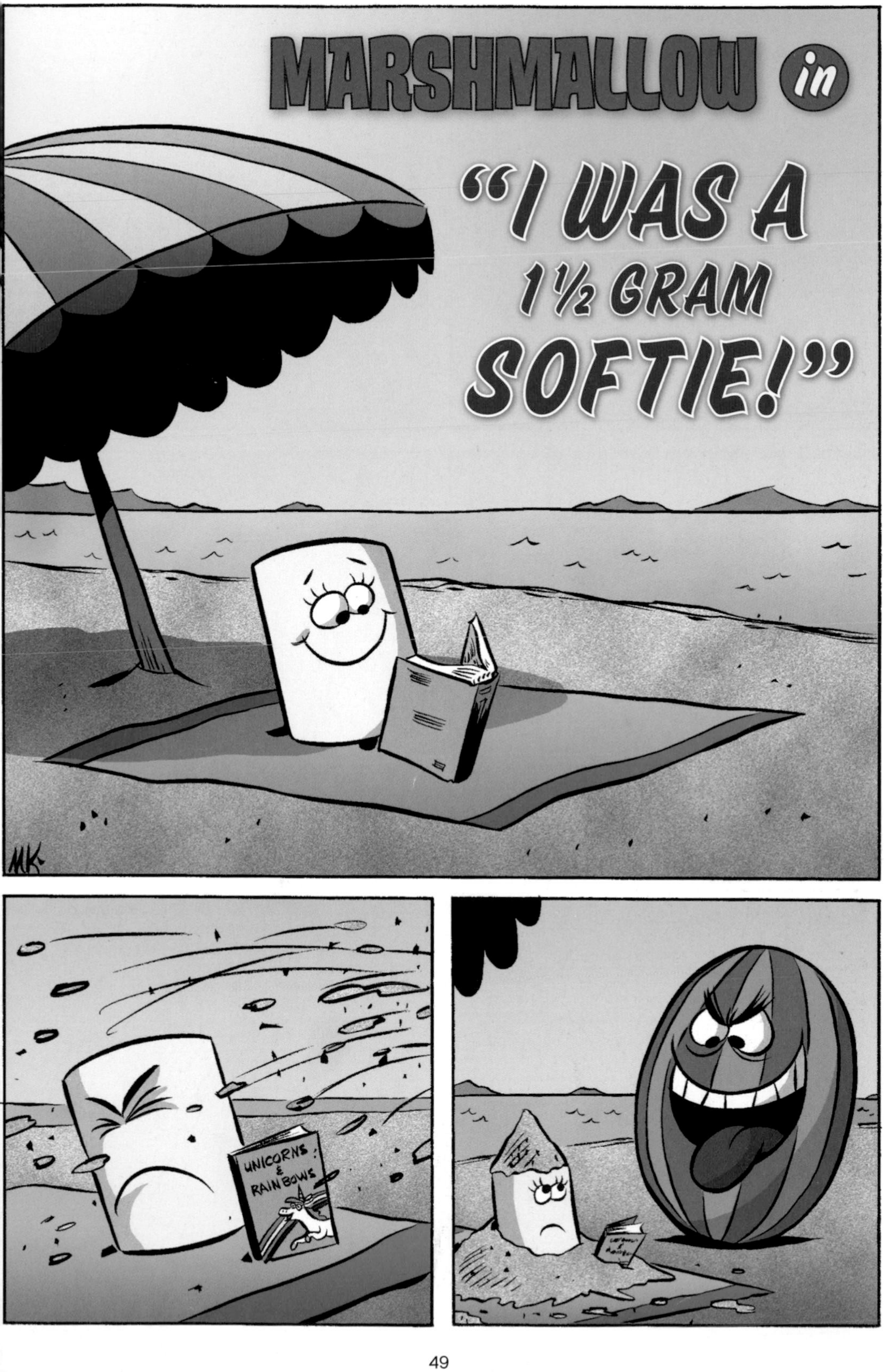
MARSHMALLOW in
“I WAS A 1½ GRAM SOFTIE!”
MK
UNICORNS & RAINBOWS

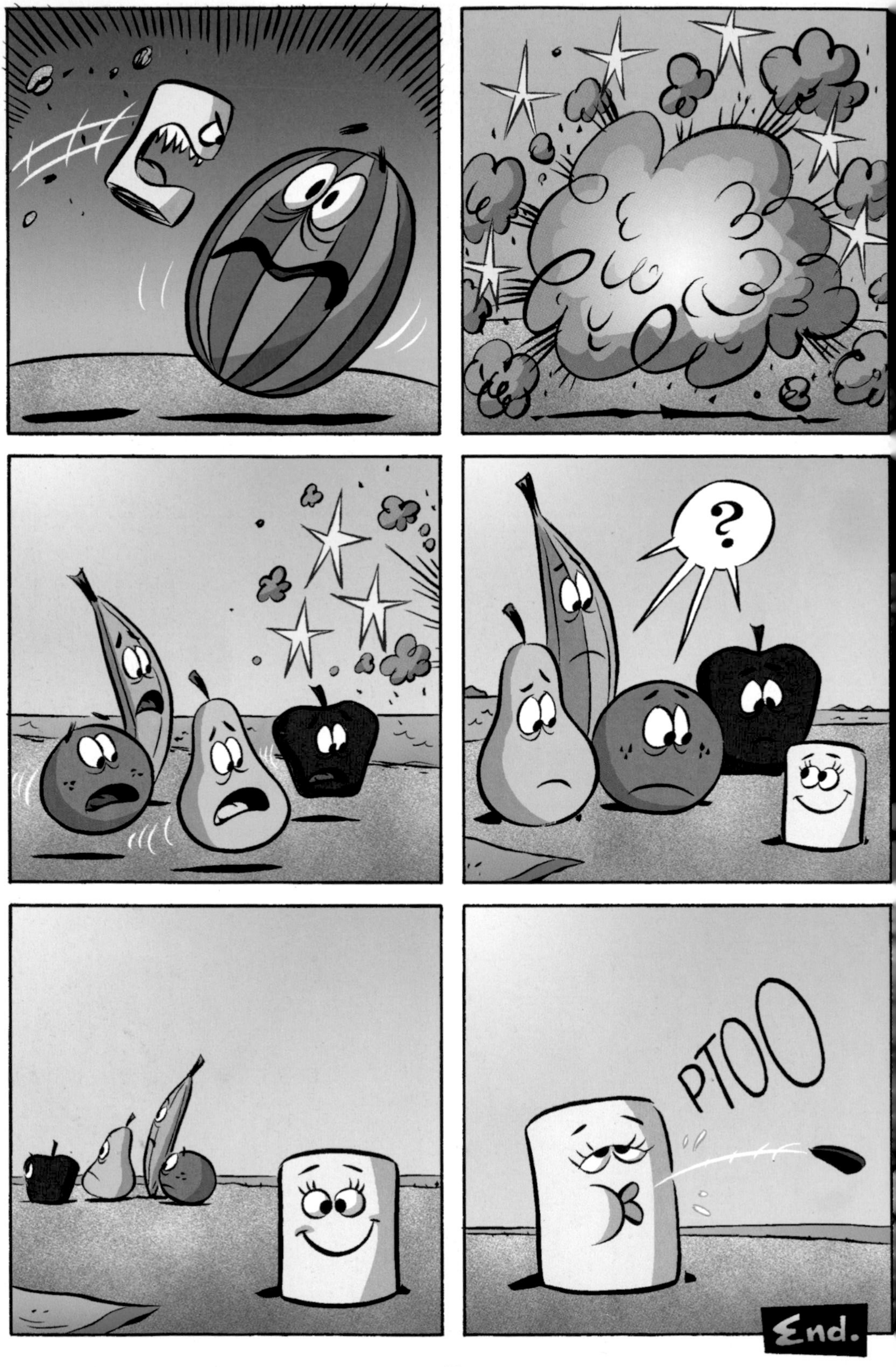
?
PTOO
End.

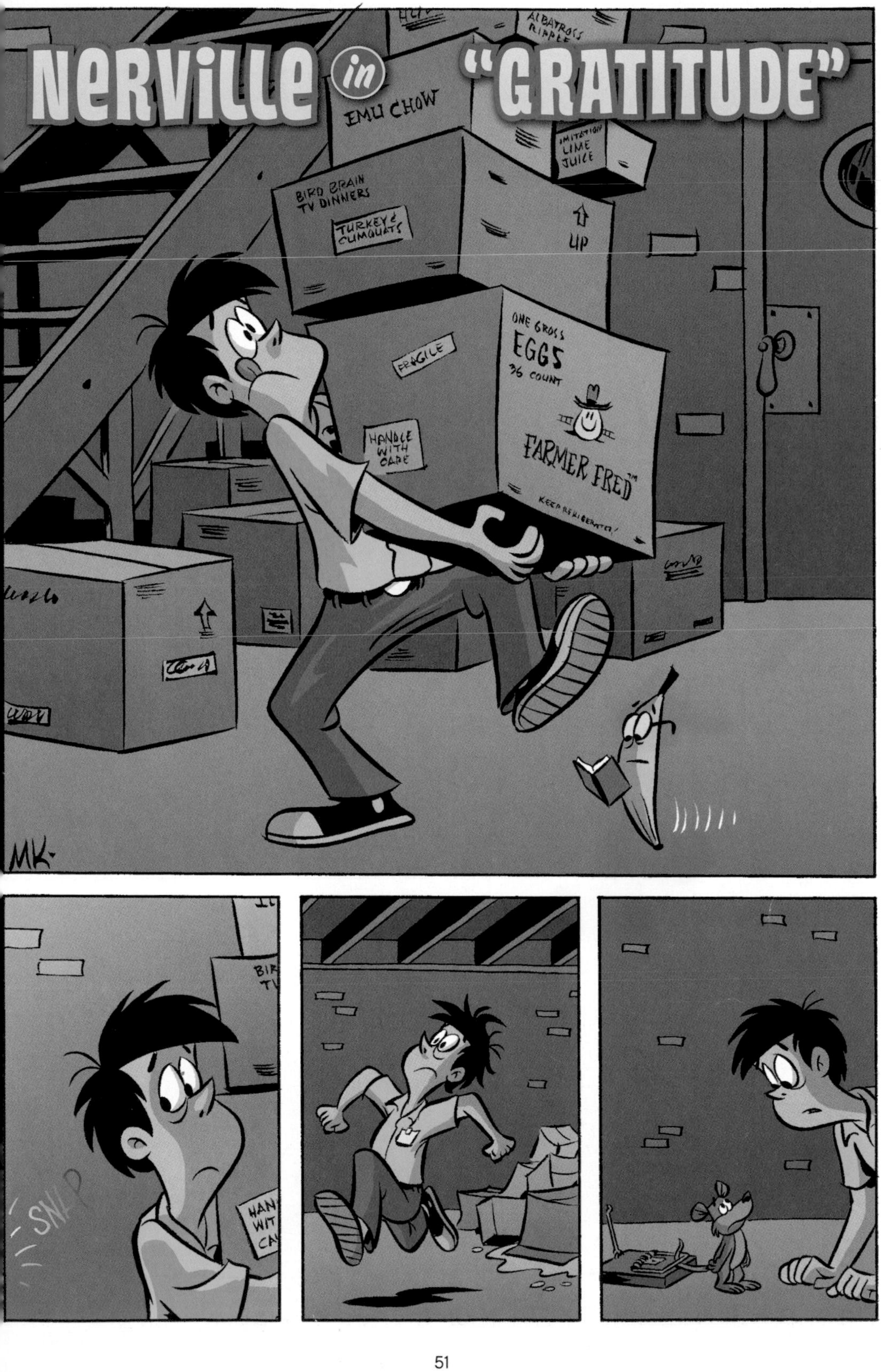

NERVILLE in "GRATITUDE"
ALBATROSS RIPPLE
EMU CHOW
IMITATION LIME JUICE
BIRD BRAIN TV DINNERS
TURKEY & CUMQUATS
UP
ONE GROSS EGGS 36 COUNT
FRAGILE
HANDLE WITH CARE
FARMER FRED™
MK
SNAP

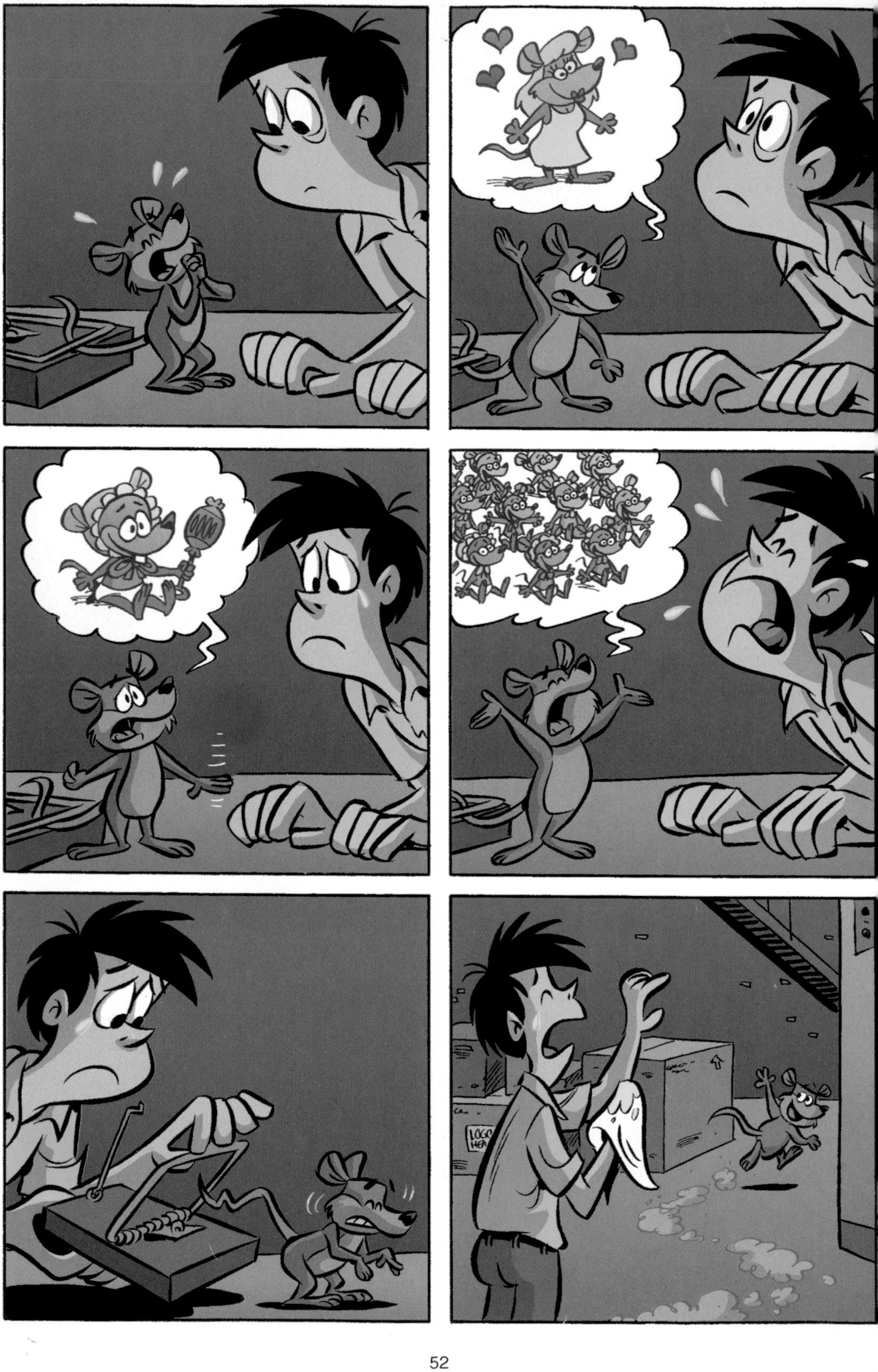

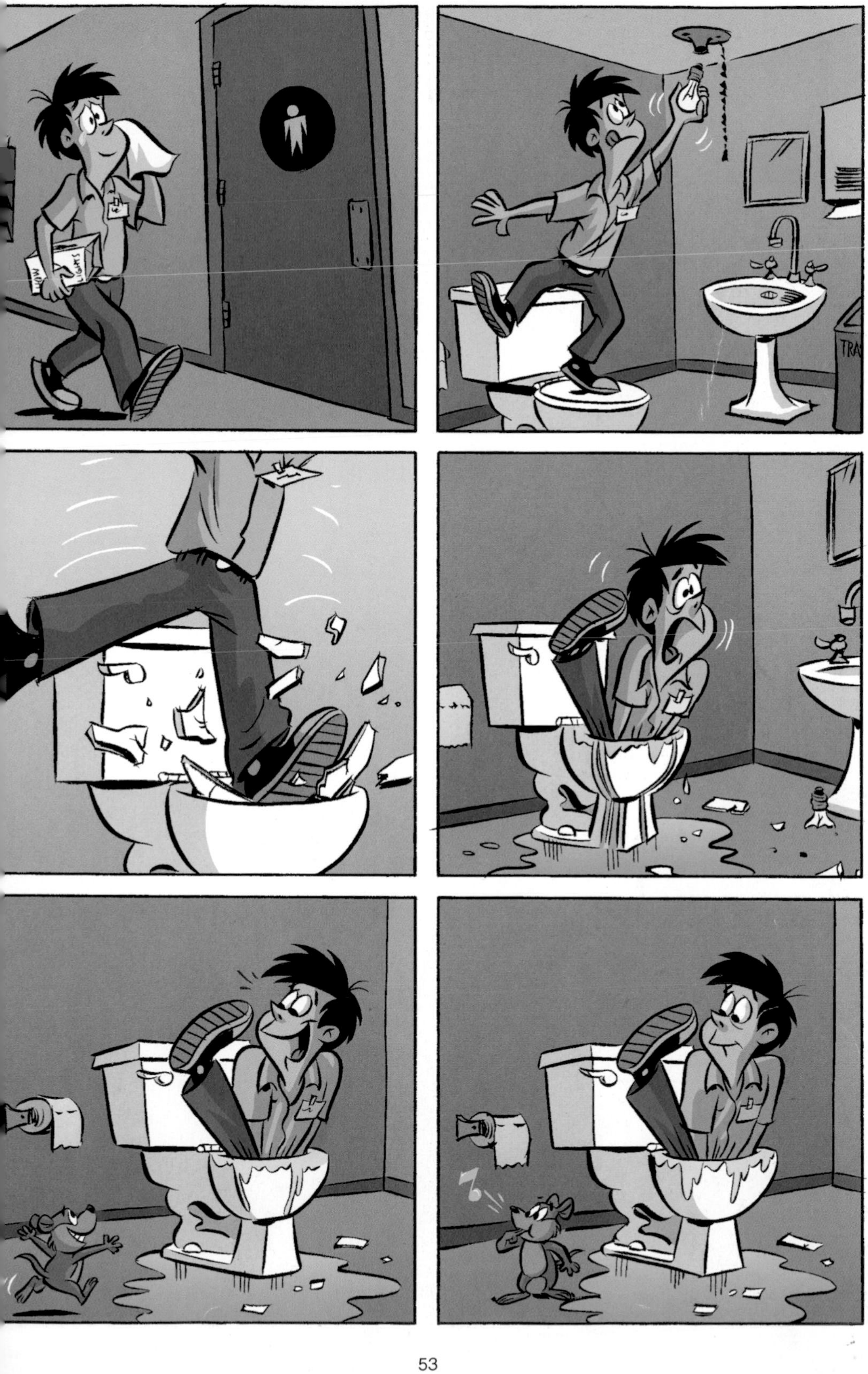
LIGHTS

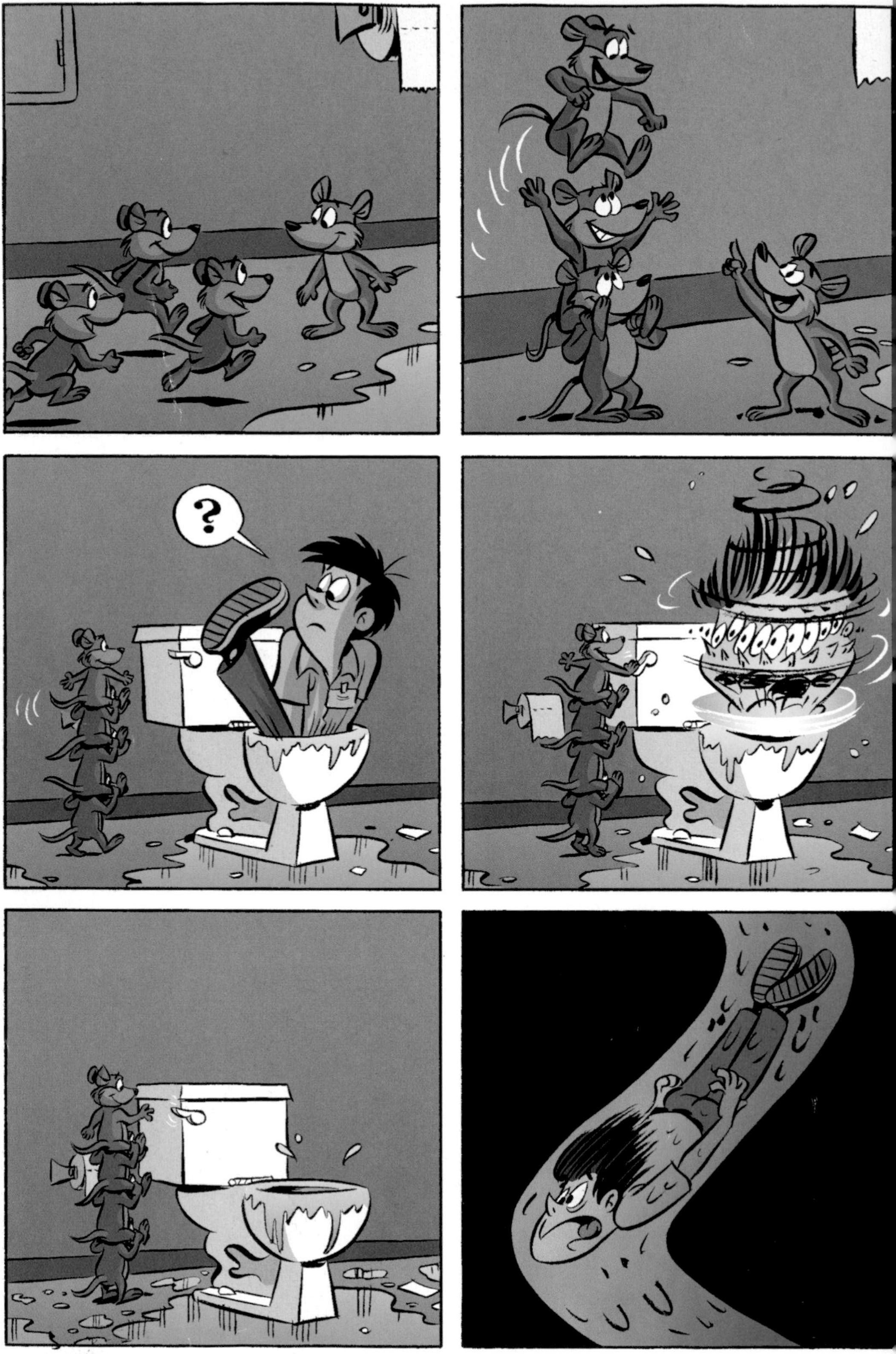
?

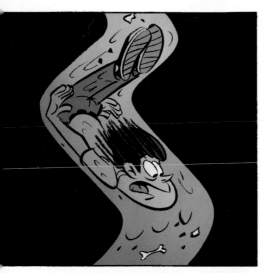

END.

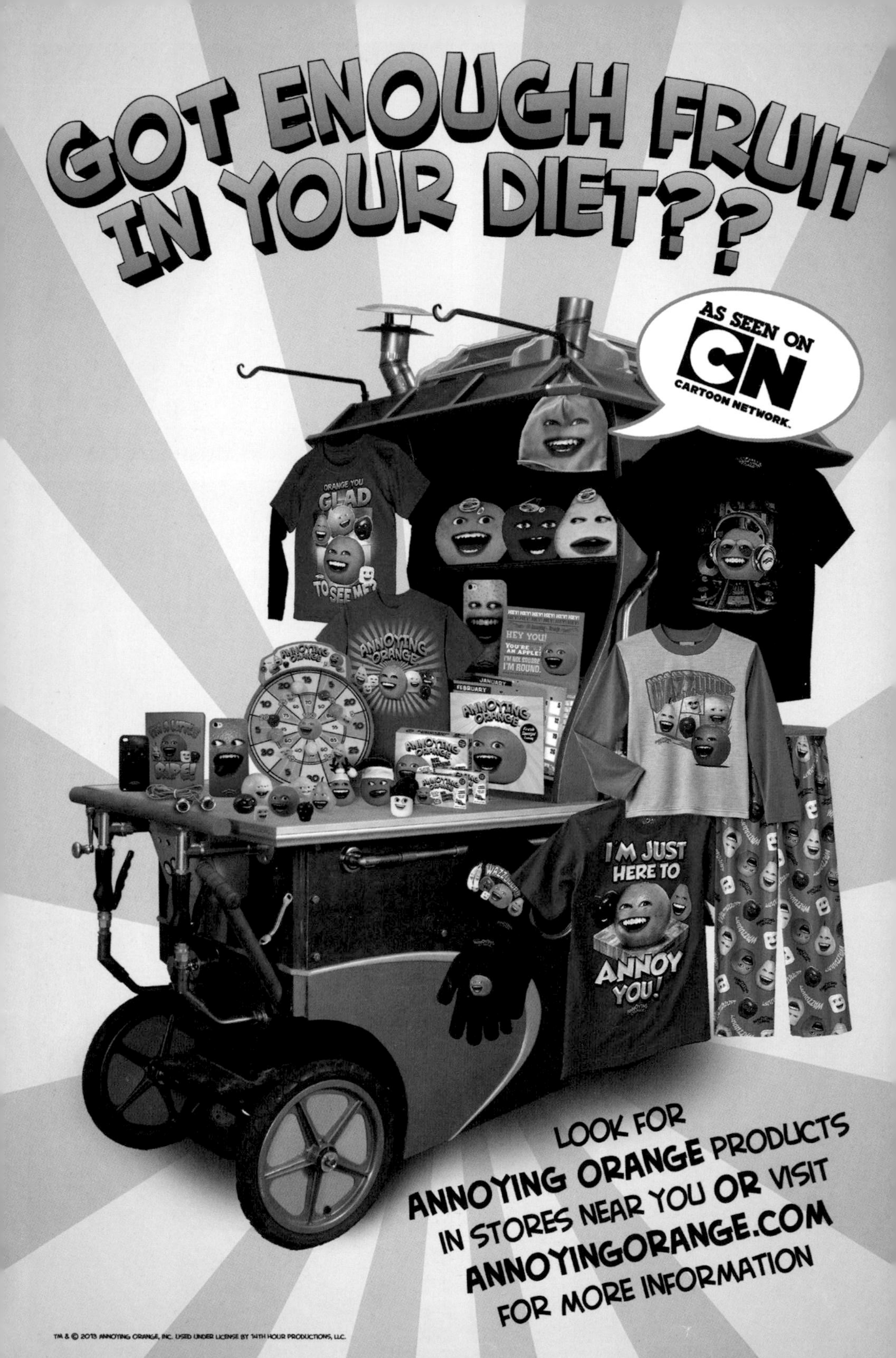

GOT ENOUGH FRUIT IN YOUR DIET??
AS SEEN ON
CN
CARTOON NETWORK.
ORANGE YOU GLAD TO SEE ME?
ANNOYING ORANGE
HEY YOU!
I'M ROUND.
I'M JUST HERE TO ANNOY YOU!
LOOK FOR
ANNOYING ORANGE PRODUCTS
IN STORES NEAR YOU OR VISIT
ANNOYINGORANGE.COM
FOR MORE INFORMATION
TM & © 2013 ANNOYING ORANGE, INC. USED UNDER LICENSE BY 14TH HOUR PRODUCTIONS, LLC.

WATCH OUT FOR PAPERCUTZ

Welcome to the fat-free, fruit-flavored fifth ANNOYING ORANGE graphic novel from Papercutz, the cantankerous commune of semi-vegetarians dedicated to publishing great graphic novels for all ages. I'm Jim Salicrup, the Editor-in-Cheap, er, I mean, Chief of this off-beat unorganized organization, and I'm here to set up the next bit, er, I mean, offer an exclusive behind-the-scenes peek at a major publishing event, and a really big surprise for everyone who picked up this very special graphic novel!

Here's the story. As we all know, Orange has become a super-huge mega-star who has triumphantly emerged from the Internet to first conquer television, with the highly-rated *The High Fructose Adventures of Annoying Orange* Cartoon Network TV series, then the best-selling DVDs of said series, and Orange is now trying to make some noise in the super-competitive, highly respected, coolest art form of all—graphic novels. While Orange thinks the world of cartoonists Mike Kazaleh and Scott Shaw!, he wanted to do something extra-special in this graphic novel. Not unlike many other major talents who first came to prominence by being funny, or in this specific case, being annoying, Orange yearns to show the world that he is capable of so much more. So, following in the footsteps of Jerry Lewis (the comic genius loved by countless sophisticated French intellectuals, who has taken on such serious roles as the late night talk show host Jerry Langford in Martin Scorsese's critically acclaimed *The King of Comedy*), Bill Murray (the Emmy award-winning cast member of *Saturday Night Live*, who was nominated for an Academy Award for his dramatic role in Sofia Coppola's *Lost in Translation*), and Steve Martin (Bill Murray's fellow "Wild and Crazy Guy" from *SNL*, super-popular stand-up comedian, he couldn't resist taking on a dramatic part in *Pennies from Heaven* after the huge success of his starring role in *The Jerk*), Orange has decided to take on perhaps the most challenging and dramatic role of his career—*Hamlet* by William Shakespeare.

For those of you looking for a punchline, I assure you, there is none. Orange is very serious about his latest challenge. Now while we love to dedicate an entire graphic novel to this no doubt impressive dramatic debut, unfortunately Papercutz has already published a comics adaptation of Hamlet in CLASSICS ILLUSTRATED #5 and we're not looking to publish another at this time. But Orange can be rather stubborn, so we worked out a compromise which should please everyone. We all agreed to let Orange perfume Hamlet's most famous soliloquy on the pages following.

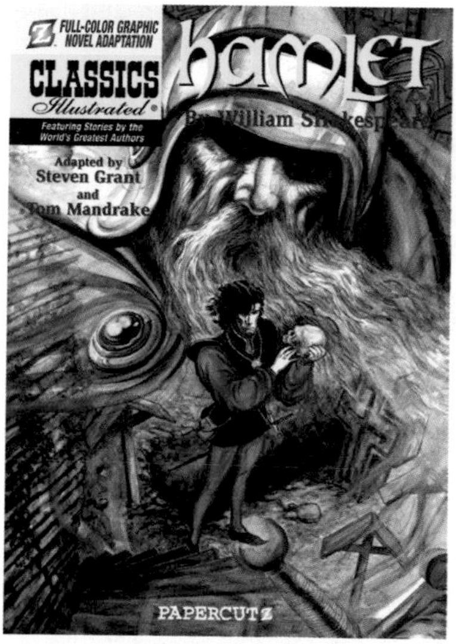

FULL-COLOR GRAPHIC NOVEL ADAPTATION
CLASSICS Illustrated
Featuring Stories by the World's Greatest Authors
Hamlet
Adapted by
Steven Grant
and
PAPERCUTZ

So, here it is! You are now cordially invited to an exclusive reading of one of Shakespeare's most unforgettable works of art, as performed by Orange. (Harvey and Eisner[1] committees please take note!) So, don't be an Apple—turn the page and prepare to be cultured!

Thanks,

Jim

STAY IN TOUCH!

EMAIL:	salicrup@papercutz.com
WEB:	papercutz.com
TWITTER:	@papercutzgn
FACEBOOK:	PAPERCUTZGRAPHICNOVELS
REGULAR MAIL:	Papercutz, 160 Broadway, Suite 700, East Wing, New York, NY 10038

[1] The comicbook world's most prestigious awards.

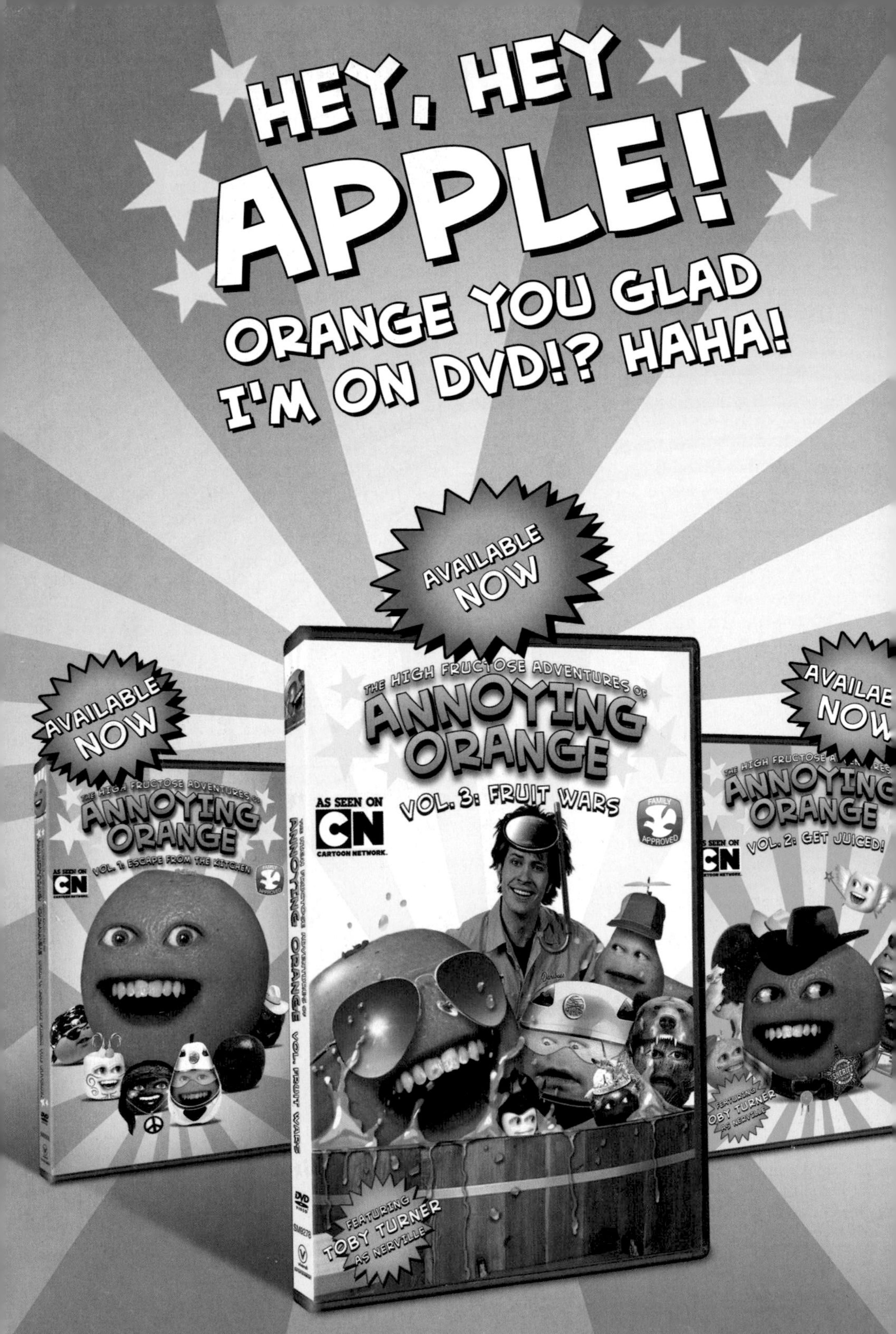
HEY, HEY
APPLE!
ORANGE YOU GLAD
I'M ON DVD!? HAHA!
AVAILABLE NOW
THE HIGH FRUCTOSE ADVENTURES OF
ANNOYING ORANGE
AS SEEN ON
CN
CARTOON NETWORK.
VOL. 3: FRUIT WARS
FAMILY APPROVED
FEATURING TOBY TURNER AS NERVILLE
VOL. 1: ESCAPE FROM THE KITCHEN
VOL. 2: GET JUICED!

HAMLET

By William Shakespeare

Performed by Orange

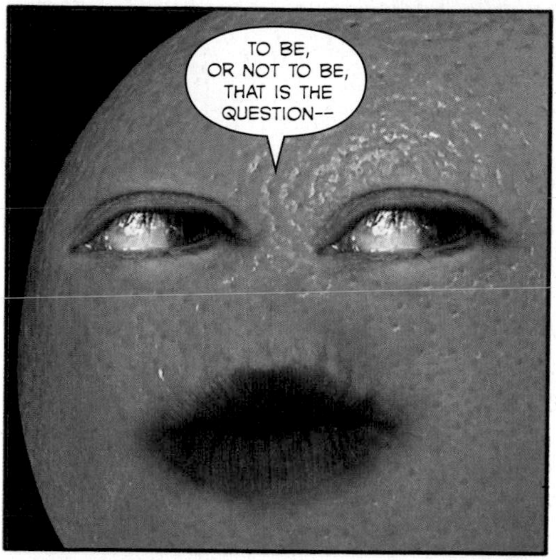
TO BE, OR NOT TO BE, THAT IS THE QUESTION--

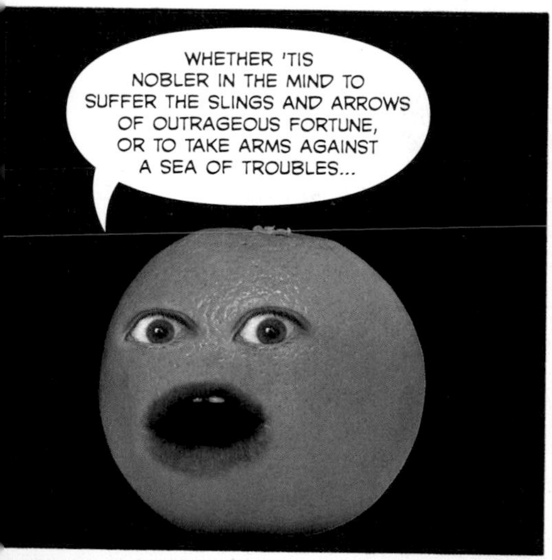
WHETHER 'TIS NOBLER IN THE MIND TO SUFFER THE SLINGS AND ARROWS OF OUTRAGEOUS FORTUNE, OR TO TAKE ARMS AGAINST A SEA OF TROUBLES...

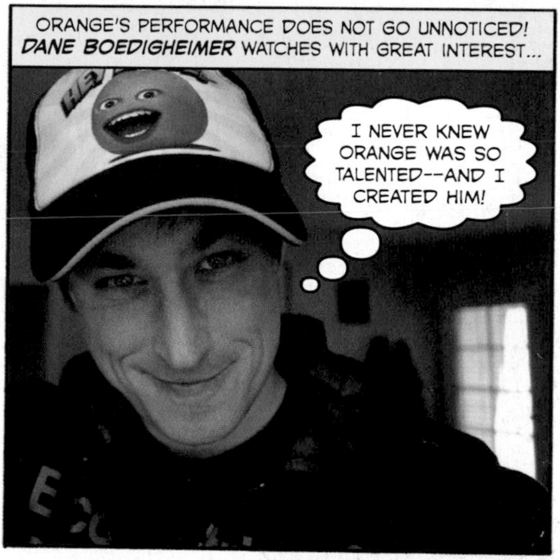
ORANGE'S PERFORMANCE DOES NOT GO UNNOTICED! *DANE BOEDIGHEIMER* WATCHES WITH GREAT INTEREST...
I NEVER KNEW ORANGE WAS SO TALENTED--AND I CREATED HIM!

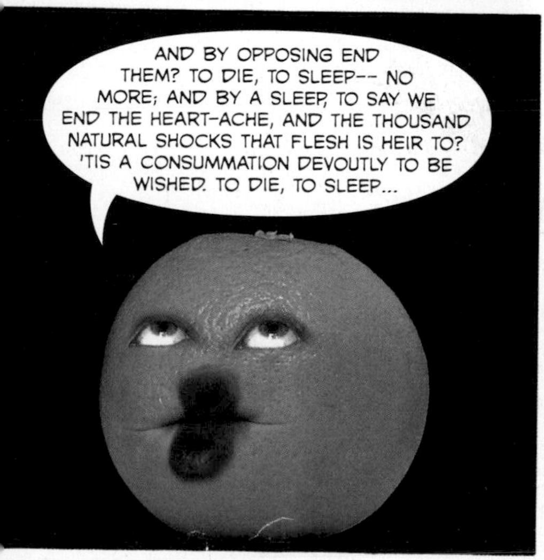
AND BY OPPOSING END THEM? TO DIE, TO SLEEP-- NO MORE; AND BY A SLEEP, TO SAY WE END THE HEART-ACHE, AND THE THOUSAND NATURAL SHOCKS THAT FLESH IS HEIR TO? 'TIS A CONSUMMATION DEVOUTLY TO BE WISHED. TO DIE, TO SLEEP...

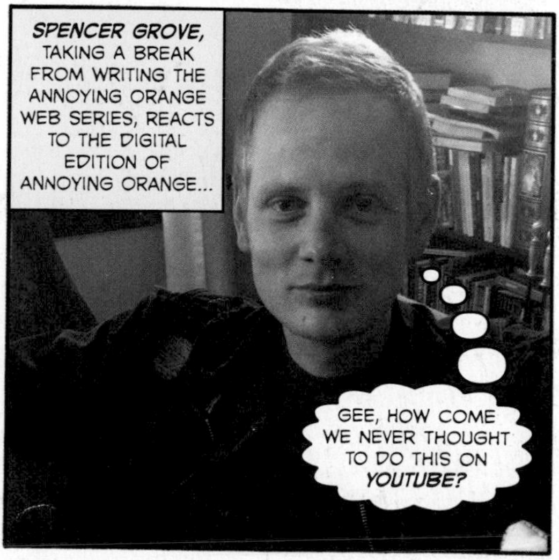
SPENCER GROVE, TAKING A BREAK FROM WRITING THE ANNOYING ORANGE WEB SERIES, REACTS TO THE DIGITAL EDITION OF ANNOYING ORANGE...
GEE, HOW COME WE NEVER THOUGHT TO DO THIS ON *YOUTUBE?*

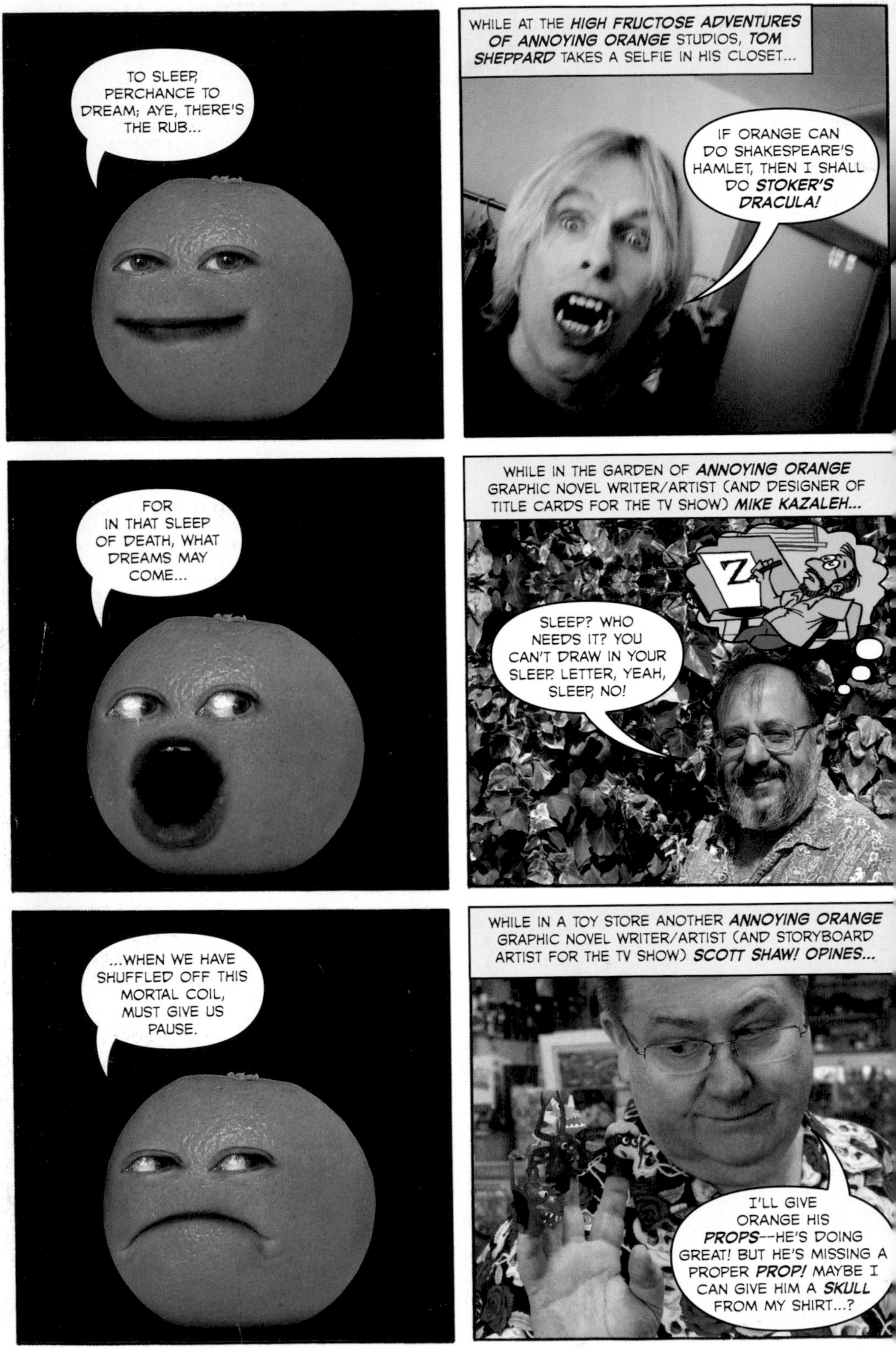
TO SLEEP, PERCHANCE TO DREAM; AYE, THERE'S THE RUB...
WHILE AT THE HIGH FRUCTOSE ADVENTURES OF ANNOYING ORANGE STUDIOS, TOM SHEPPARD TAKES A SELFIE IN HIS CLOSET...
IF ORANGE CAN DO SHAKESPEARE'S HAMLET, THEN I SHALL DO STOKER'S DRACULA!
FOR IN THAT SLEEP OF DEATH, WHAT DREAMS MAY COME...
WHILE IN THE GARDEN OF ANNOYING ORANGE GRAPHIC NOVEL WRITER/ARTIST (AND DESIGNER OF TITLE CARDS FOR THE TV SHOW) MIKE KAZALEH...
SLEEP? WHO NEEDS IT? YOU CAN'T DRAW IN YOUR SLEEP. LETTER, YEAH, SLEEP, NO!
...WHEN WE HAVE SHUFFLED OFF THIS MORTAL COIL, MUST GIVE US PAUSE.
WHILE IN A TOY STORE ANOTHER ANNOYING ORANGE GRAPHIC NOVEL WRITER/ARTIST (AND STORYBOARD ARTIST FOR THE TV SHOW) SCOTT SHAW! OPINES...
I'LL GIVE ORANGE HIS PROPS--HE'S DOING GREAT! BUT HE'S MISSING A PROPER PROP! MAYBE I CAN GIVE HIM A SKULL FROM MY SHIRT...?

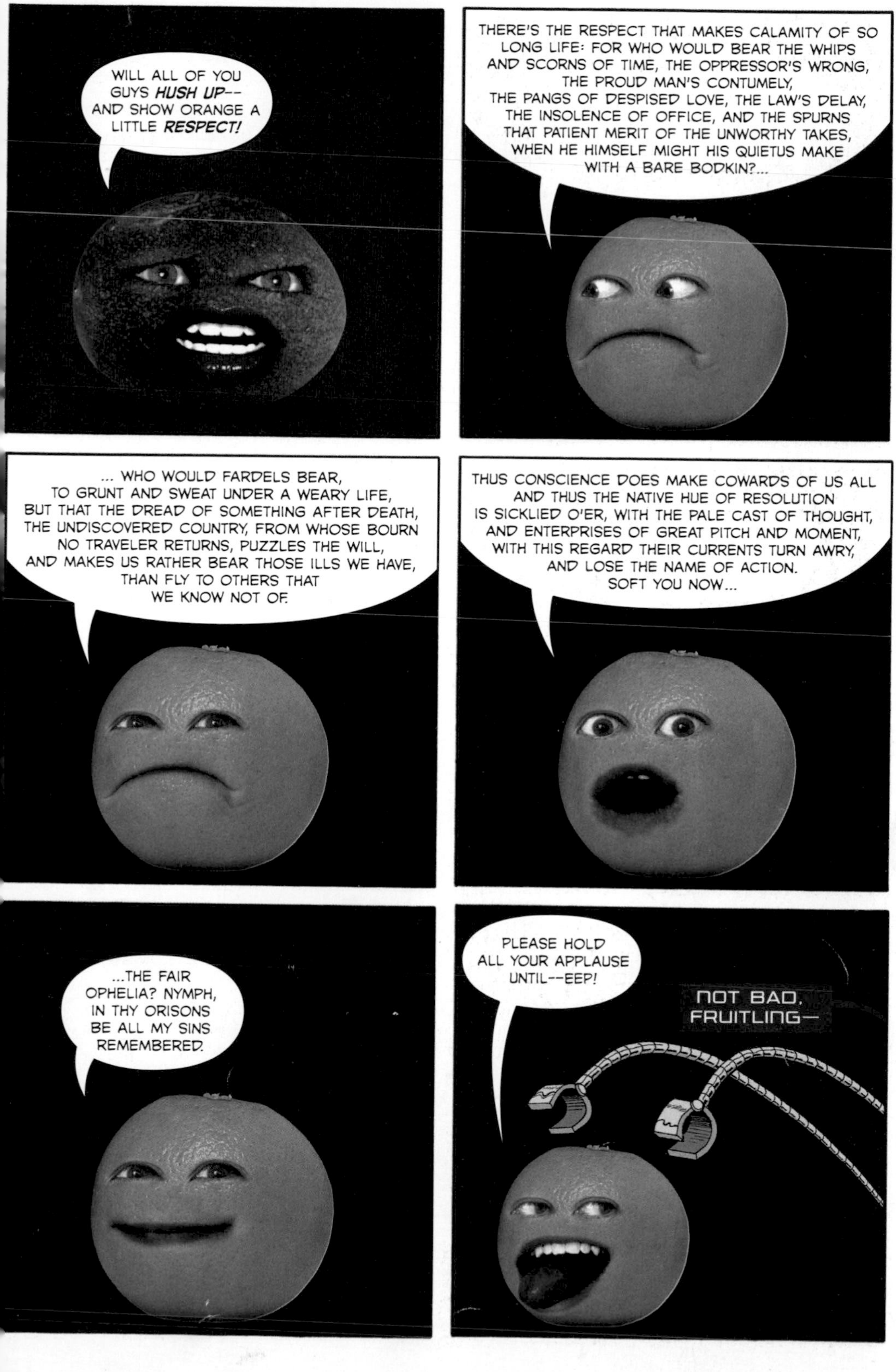
WILL ALL OF YOU GUYS *HUSH UP*-- AND SHOW ORANGE A LITTLE *RESPECT!*
THERE'S THE RESPECT THAT MAKES CALAMITY OF SO LONG LIFE: FOR WHO WOULD BEAR THE WHIPS AND SCORNS OF TIME, THE OPPRESSOR'S WRONG, THE PROUD MAN'S CONTUMELY, THE PANGS OF DESPISED LOVE, THE LAW'S DELAY, THE INSOLENCE OF OFFICE, AND THE SPURNS THAT PATIENT MERIT OF THE UNWORTHY TAKES, WHEN HE HIMSELF MIGHT HIS QUIETUS MAKE WITH A BARE BODKIN?...
... WHO WOULD FARDELS BEAR, TO GRUNT AND SWEAT UNDER A WEARY LIFE, BUT THAT THE DREAD OF SOMETHING AFTER DEATH, THE UNDISCOVERED COUNTRY, FROM WHOSE BOURN NO TRAVELER RETURNS, PUZZLES THE WILL, AND MAKES US RATHER BEAR THOSE ILLS WE HAVE, THAN FLY TO OTHERS THAT WE KNOW NOT OF.
THUS CONSCIENCE DOES MAKE COWARDS OF US ALL AND THUS THE NATIVE HUE OF RESOLUTION IS SICKLIED O'ER, WITH THE PALE CAST OF THOUGHT, AND ENTERPRISES OF GREAT PITCH AND MOMENT, WITH THIS REGARD THEIR CURRENTS TURN AWRY, AND LOSE THE NAME OF ACTION. SOFT YOU NOW...
...THE FAIR OPHELIA? NYMPH, IN THY ORISONS BE ALL MY SINS REMEMBERED.
PLEASE HOLD ALL YOUR APPLAUSE UNTIL--EEP!
NOT BAD, FRUITLING—

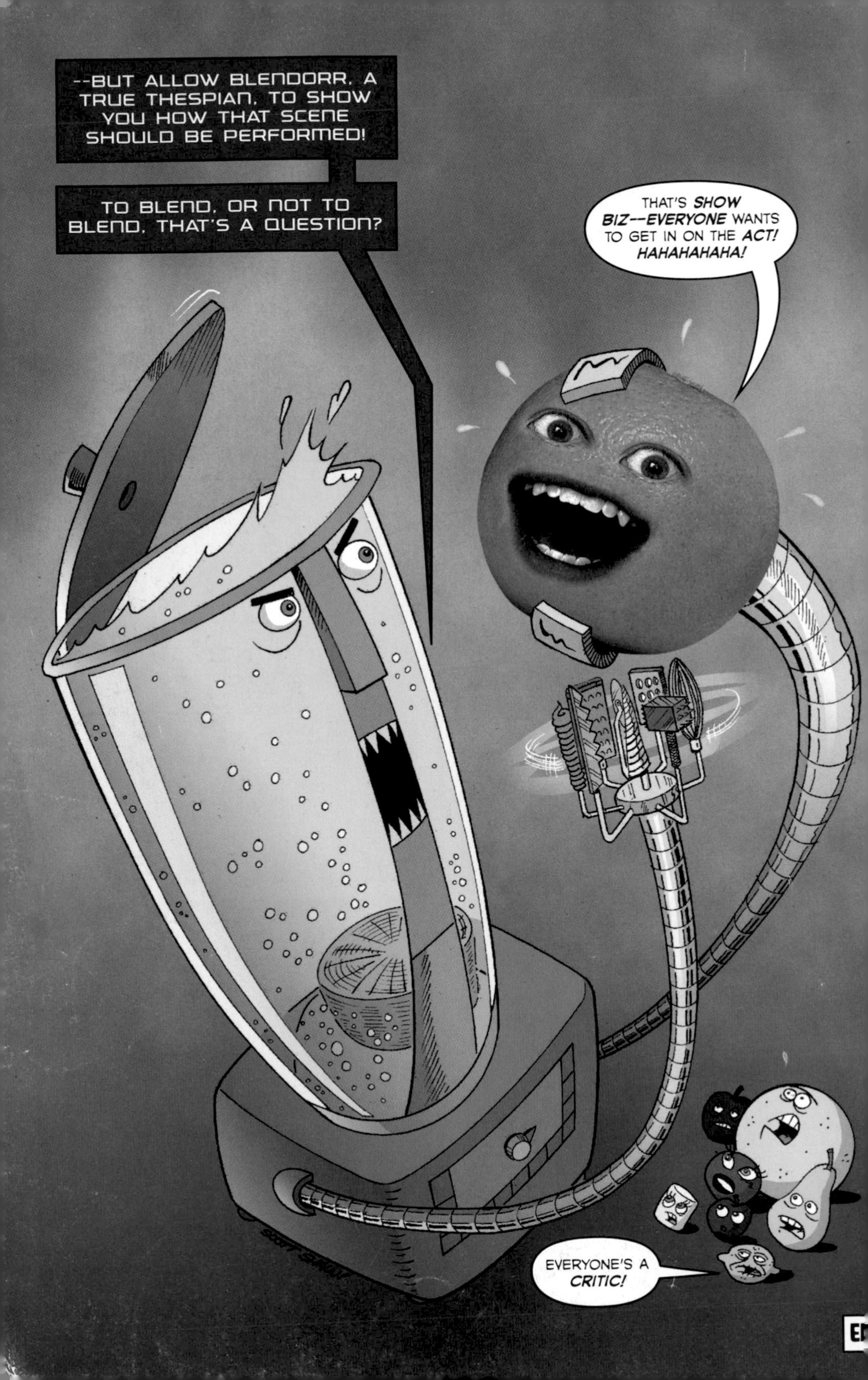
--BUT ALLOW BLENDORR, A TRUE THESPIAN, TO SHOW YOU HOW THAT SCENE SHOULD BE PERFORMED!
TO BLEND, OR NOT TO BLEND, THAT'S A QUESTION?
THAT'S SHOW BIZ--EVERYONE WANTS TO GET IN ON THE ACT! HAHAHAHAHA!
EVERYONE'S A CRITIC!

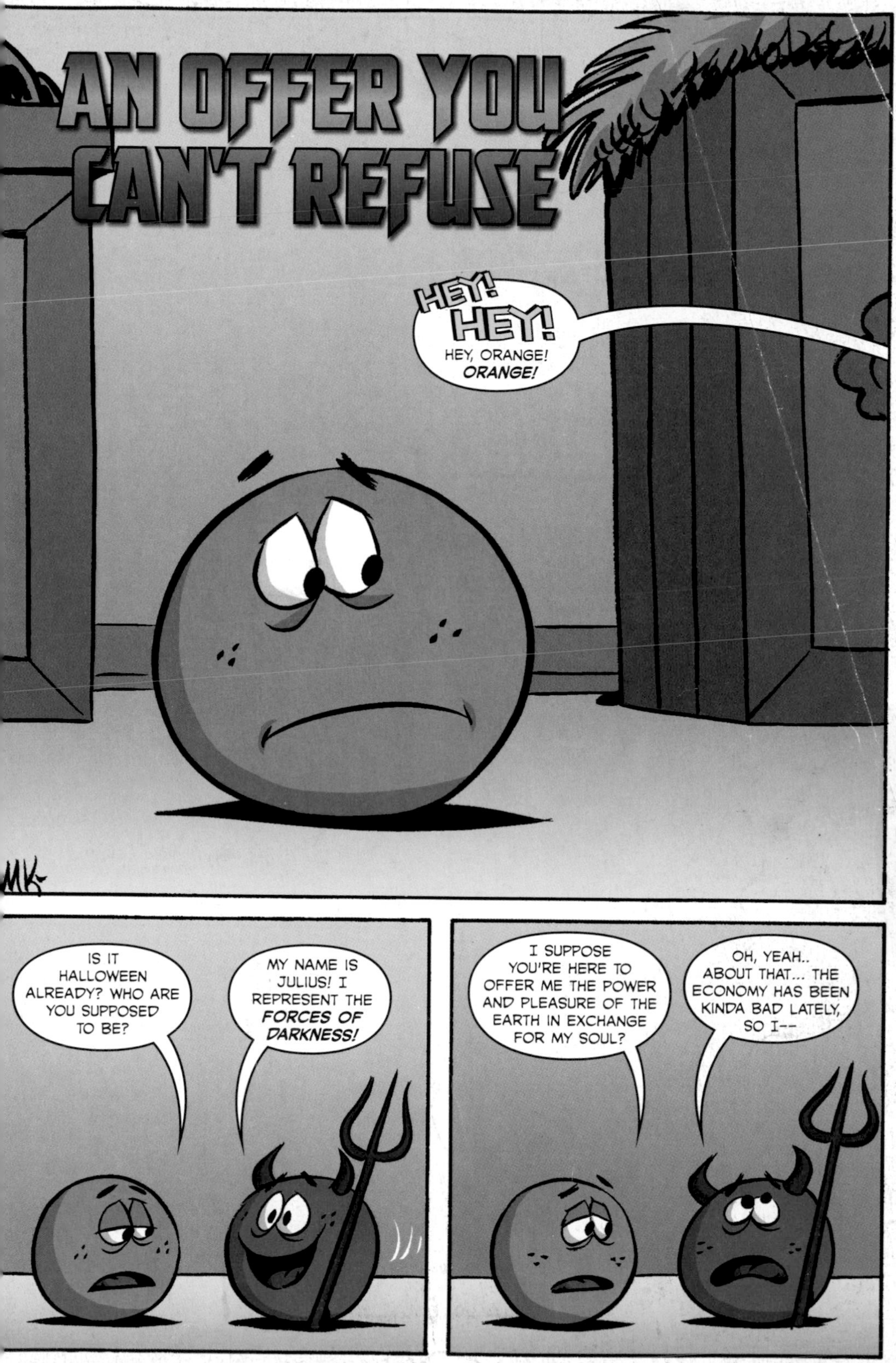
AN OFFER YOU CAN'T REFUSE
HEY! HEY! HEY, ORANGE! *ORANGE!*
MK
IS IT HALLOWEEN ALREADY? WHO ARE YOU SUPPOSED TO BE?
MY NAME IS JULIUS! I REPRESENT THE *FORCES OF DARKNESS!*
I SUPPOSE YOU'RE HERE TO OFFER ME THE POWER AND PLEASURE OF THE EARTH IN EXCHANGE FOR MY SOUL?
OH, YEAH.. ABOUT THAT... THE ECONOMY HAS BEEN KINDA BAD LATELY, SO I--

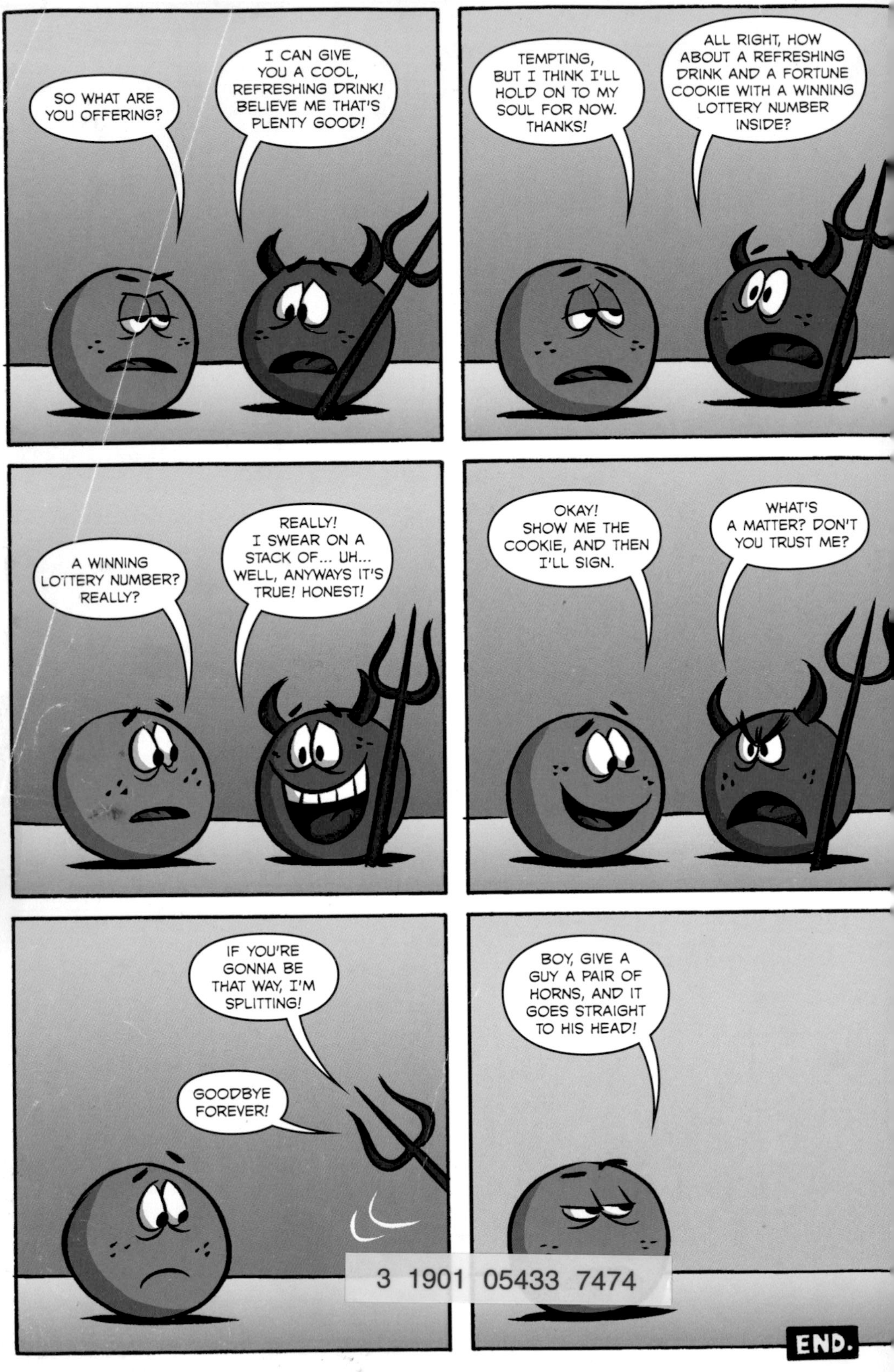
SO WHAT ARE YOU OFFERING?
I CAN GIVE YOU A COOL, REFRESHING DRINK! BELIEVE ME THAT'S PLENTY GOOD!
TEMPTING, BUT I THINK I'LL HOLD ON TO MY SOUL FOR NOW. THANKS!
ALL RIGHT, HOW ABOUT A REFRESHING DRINK AND A FORTUNE COOKIE WITH A WINNING LOTTERY NUMBER INSIDE?
A WINNING LOTTERY NUMBER? REALLY?
REALLY! I SWEAR ON A STACK OF... UH... WELL, ANYWAYS IT'S TRUE! HONEST!
OKAY! SHOW ME THE COOKIE, AND THEN I'LL SIGN.
WHAT'S A MATTER? DON'T YOU TRUST ME?
IF YOU'RE GONNA BE THAT WAY, I'M SPLITTING!
GOODBYE FOREVER!
BOY, GIVE A GUY A PAIR OF HORNS, AND IT GOES STRAIGHT TO HIS HEAD!
END.